The Hockey Detective

By: J. G. McBreen

ISBN-13: 978-0615948232
ISBN-10: 0615948235

Tralee Publishers, Chicago, Illinois

Unless you try to do something beyond what you have already mastered, you will never grow.

Ralph Waldo Emerson

Chapter 1

Logan Michaud heard the soft rap on his bedroom door just seconds before its hinges creaked and his mother's face appeared in the crack.

"Are you awake, Logan?" she asked. "We need to get to the school early to register."

"Just getting up, Mom," he answered. And then hearing her footsteps recede down the hallway, he rolled over on his side and faced the wall instead.

Moments later the sound of nails scratching on the wood floor drew closer and a wet nose buried itself in his face.

"Hey, buddy," he murmured.

He reached up and scratched Joker behind the ear. "Why is it that you're always in a good mood?" he asked. "Even at six-fifteen in the morning."

The brown and black shepherd-collie mix answered by dragging his tongue across Logan's cheek.

"Great," he chuckled. "Now if you lick the other side, I won't have to shower today."

Forty-five minutes later Logan and his mom were seated in the office of Mrs. Lisa Greene, principal of West Bend Middle School.

"So, as I was saying, we'll start Logan in these classes temporarily and after we see how he does on his placement exams, we'll make any necessary adjustments," Mrs. Greene said. "I've never had a transfer student from Canada before, so I can't say I'm familiar with your country's educational system."

"Logan's always been a very good student," his mom replied. "I'm hoping it'll be a smooth transition."

Just then a pretty blond, blue-eyed girl with her hair pulled back in a ponytail stuck her head into the room.

"You wanted to see me, Mrs. Greene?" she asked.

"Yes, Megan, come in."

"Megan is one of our student ambassadors," Mrs. Greene explained. "And since Logan is new to the school, I thought maybe she could show him around, make sure he gets to his classes on time."

"Sure," Megan Sweeney said, glancing over at the scowling dark-haired boy who sat slumped in a chair, his eyes fixed to the ground.

"I'd be happy to."

Suddenly a shrill bell sounded and the pounding of feet could be heard in the hallway outside. Megan quickly grabbed Logan's schedule and took off down the hall, checking once over her shoulder to be sure she was being followed. A sullen Logan trailed dejectedly behind her.

"Don't worry, Mrs. Michaud," the principal said reassuringly. "He'll be fine."

At the end of five periods, Logan and Megan entered a noisy lunchroom and Megan made a beeline for a table in the back corner.

"Ryan," she said, tapping a blond boy on the shoulder. "This is Logan. It's his first day. Can he sit with you guys for lunch?"

Megan turned back toward Logan. "This is my brother, Ryan. I'll be back to take you to your seventh period class," and with that Megan abruptly turned on her heel and walked away.

Logan could feel the warm flush of embarrassment creep up the back of his neck as six pairs of eyes turned expectantly toward him. There was a moment of silence and then Ryan lightly shoved the guy seated next to him, "C'mon, Tyler, don't be a jerk. Move over."

"Have a seat," he said to Logan as he nodded to the open space beside him.

Logan stiffly swung his legs over the bench and sat down.

Ryan peeked into the brown lunch bag in front of him and groaned. "No matter how many times I tell my mom, no baloney, what do I get? You guessed it, baloney!"

"Anyone wanna hit the lunch line?" he asked.

Ryan turned to Logan, "Did you bring something with you or do you want to check out the cafeteria?"

Logan knew he had a peanut butter sandwich in his backpack, but it wasn't really his favorite. "I don't have any money on me," he replied.

4

"Don't need it. All you need is your ID card and if that doesn't work, I'll front you," Ryan said.

Logan retrieved his ID card from the front flap of his backpack and followed Ryan over to cafeteria line A.

"Line A is for the ala carte items, like hamburgers and pizza. Line B is for the lunch meals. Here's a tip – avoid Line B at all costs," Ryan said, grinning.

Standing in line next to Ryan Sweeney, Logan noticed they were almost the same height, except whereas Ryan was blond and tanned, Logan was dark-haired and pale. Ryan was muscular under his t-shirt, as Logan was, and looked like an athlete.

"So where are you from?" Ryan asked.

"Winnipeg, Canada."

"No kidding." Ryan's brows arched. "Do you play hockey?"

"I did . . . back home," Logan answered, hesitating slightly and looking away.

The subtle change in Logan's demeanor was lost on Ryan who launched instead into a description of West Bend's local hockey club, the Warriors.

"Our club is newer and smaller than some of the other clubs around, but we're growing and always looking for new players," he said excitedly. "We haven't had the best track record, but every year we seem to improve. Tryouts start on Friday. You should come out. What position did you play?"

"Right wing, mostly. Some defense."

When they got back to the table with their hamburgers and chips, Ryan filled the other guys in on Logan's experience playing hockey in Canada. It turned out that most of Logan's new tablemates were hockey players on the Warriors' Pee Wee team, with the exception of one older boy who played at the Bantam level.

"You know, every Wednesday night they have Rat Ice over at the rink from 4:30 to 6:00 p.m." Ryan said. "They put the Pee Wees and Bantams together, but there's no checking. You should stop by and check out the competition. It's only $10, no pads, helmets only."

Just then the warning bell rang and Megan came to collect Logan for his next class.

"I'll think about it," Logan promised, as he hurried off after Megan who was already out the lunchroom door.

Chapter 2

The next few days flew by. Logan spent two lunch periods in a row hunched over a desk in an empty classroom taking placement tests in math and English.

He passed Ryan in the hall a couple of times and the other boy acknowledged him with a smile and a nod. Once he called out, "Don't forget about Wednesday night, Rat Ice, 4:30, be there!"

When Logan told his mom, she was encouraging but cautious.

"It sounds like a wonderful idea," she said "but, you know, hockey in the United States is much more expensive than it is in Canada."

"At least that's what I've heard ..." she said softly, her voice trailing off.

The two of them were seated at the small table in the kitchen with dirty dishes from the night's dinner scattered in front of them. Joker was lying quietly at Logan's feet, his belly full of table scraps. A warm September breeze gently lifted the curtains of the open window over the sink.

"I know it's what your father would have wanted," his mom continued, a slight catch in her throat.

Before his mom could avert her eyes, Logan saw the tears welling up, ready to spill over, and he silently cursed himself.

These last six months had been hard on both of them. First, there was the shock of his father's death. Trying to get home for Valentine's Day during a blizzard, his father had lost control of his car and skidded off a slippery road. One day he was there and the next he was simply gone, a memory. His father's booming voice and larger than life 6' 3" presence had filled their lives and his absence left an enormous hole. The silence in the house had been suffocating.

His mom told him they needed to move back to the States because she wasn't able to find a job in

Canada. And she wanted to be closer to her parents – his grandparents. But Logan knew it was more than that. He knew that everything about Canada reminded her of his father. The move to Illinois represented a new start, a new beginning. She had seemed happier too since they had arrived. He no longer heard the muffled sounds of her crying herself to sleep every night.

Logan reached across the table and covered his mom's hand with his own.

"I know, Mom," he said gently. "It's okay if I don't play this year. Maybe I can get a part-time job and save some money for next year."

"In the meantime," he continued, "Rat Ice is only $10 a session and it will help me keep my skills up."

His mother's face brightened a little. "Yes, and maybe I can set some money aside and talk to your grandparents," she said.

Logan stepped out of his back door and into the bright afternoon sunlight. His helmet, skates and gloves were slung over one shoulder and tucked under his other arm were his hockey stick and a skateboard.

Joker bounded on ahead, stopping to sniff every bush and tree in his path.

The back edge of the yard bordered dense woods that screened a view of an industrial park on the other side. Logan cut through the woods, winding his way around fallen logs and thick underbrush, and emerged onto a roadway that ran parallel to the woods' north end.

Directly across from him was the last building of the industrial park. The end unit of the building had its garage doors down, and the sign above the door read "Exotic Auto Repair" in fancy gold letters. Unlike the other units, this one had a large chain-link fence encircling the driveway and a side yard, with barbed wire running across the top of the fence.

Logan dropped his skateboard and whistled for Joker. He headed west and then turned right at the end of the block, rolled another two blocks until he reached Pioneer Street, and made a left turn. The ice rink was one block further down on the southwest corner of Pioneer and Vine.

Up close the ice rink building was unimpressive. A low one-story structure built of cinder blocks and corrugated metal and surrounded by a parking lot, it was old and dilapidated. Despite a fresh coat of white paint, it had definitely seen better days.

Logan gave his money to the rink manager and asked him to keep an eye on Joker. He could hear voices coming from Locker Room 1, the first door just inside the rink area.

"Well, look who decided to show up, eh," Tyler Grayson said in a slightly mocking tone, giving his best impersonation of a fake Canadian accent.

Logan sat down on the bench and started lacing up his skates. The inside of the locker room was no better than the rest of the building. Deep gouges and graffiti covered almost every inch of the walls. *No doubt put there by angry players after a tough loss*, he thought.

He wasn't sure what he had done to deserve it, but Logan sensed Tyler didn't like him. There had been something there from the very first day, not open hostility, just an undercurrent of tension.

Across from Logan sat Carlos Fuentes, a compact and solidly built player with brown eyes and a ready smile. Next to him, Dylan Van Kampen, another member of the Pee Wee squad, was winding thick black tape around the bottom of his stick. It looked as if Ryan hadn't arrived at the rink yet.

Logan stepped out on the ice and began gliding slowly with long, even strides, just trying to get a feel for the surface. It had been months since he had skated. Gradually, he began to pick up speed, one leg smoothly crossing over the other. He twisted and turned, skating backwards and weaving in and out of other skaters, eventually skidding to a stop in front of the players' bench.

There he dropped to the ice and started stretching. One knee down and the other leg straight out as he slowly lowered himself as far as he could go. Then he repeated the process with the other leg.

Fweeet! An older man wearing a black Warriors jacket blew a whistle and motioned the skaters over to the boards.

"Okay, guys, we have 15 here today, so let's divide you up."

He started tossing bright yellow mesh jerseys to several of the players.

"Hey, new guy," he called, his eyes coming to rest on Logan. "You offense or defense?"

"Offense," Logan replied, reaching up to catch the yellow shirt with the number 30 on it that was summarily launched at him.

"Remember," the man said. "No checking. Keep it clean. Let's not knock somebody out with an injury before the season's even started."

Logan wriggled into his jersey while the first set of six skaters took the ice. He noticed that Tyler was on the opposing black team, playing defense.

Because of the limited number of players, they were playing 3-on-3, a faster version of the game with more shots and less defense. Although in theory one guy was supposed to hang back around center ice to guard against breakaways, in reality everyone was trying to score. The minute someone got the puck on his stick, he took off toward the opposite goal. And whoever had the puck was immediately swarmed by the other team. The goalies saw a lot of action.

After just a minute and a half, as the first lines left the ice, the score was already 1 – 0 in favor of the black team. Logan skated out with the second group of players. Behind him, James Toth, a big defenseman, dropped back to his customary spot, Dylan moved over to play left wing, and Logan drifted to the right.

The Warriors coach who was supervising didn't bother with a face-off; he just threw the puck out onto center ice. Carlos picked it up and started moving swiftly along the left boards. Dylan raced over and slapped at the puck trying to jostle it loose. It skidded sideways and Logan, who had positioned himself perfectly, was right there to grab it. He took off toward the opposite goal – only two black jerseys between him and the net.

The first black jersey was skating up to meet Logan at the blue line. It seemed as if they were on a collision course, but seconds before contact Logan feinted left and then whirled counterclockwise in a complete 360, abruptly changing direction and leaving the other player leaning the wrong way. The player flailed helplessly with his stick but it was too late. Logan was already halfway to the goal.

The second black jersey was racing along side Logan trying to intercept him before he reached the goalie. But Logan accelerated with a burst of speed that left the other guy half a length behind. Charging toward the right side of the crease, Logan twisted slightly and then angled a shot over the goalie's other shoulder. Goal!

The entire sequence had taken less than 15 seconds.

The Warriors coach in the box stared open-mouthed at the ice.

Chapter 3

"Yeah!"

Logan turned and saw Ryan, a big smile on his face, stepping onto the rink through the rink door along the boards. Ryan skated over to the bench and quickly donned a yellow jersey.

"Nice shot," he said when Logan's line returned to the side.

"Thanks."

Ryan rotated into the line-up, and after 45 minutes of play, the yellow team led 12 to 5 – with Logan responsible for 7 of his team's goals. Flying around the ice, he somehow managed to always be in the right spot at the right time. It was almost as if the puck knew how to find *him*. And once the puck landed on Logan's stick, he would break for the other net, dodging bodies with swift, precise turns and shooting with unerring accuracy.

After a while, frustration started to build on the black team. Following one series where Logan made a last second pass to Ryan who slapped it in for a score, Tyler slammed his stick to the ground in anger.

Two shifts later as Logan swept past Tyler at his team's blue line, the other boy reached out and hooked him, sending Logan crashing shoulder first into the boards.

The shrill sound of a whistle pierced the air.

"Grayson!" the coach yelled. "Over here. Now."

Logan was slow getting up, testing his limbs and joints to be sure everything was still working properly. Then he slowly made his way back to the bench.

"You okay?" Carlos asked, and Logan nodded in the affirmative.

"Watch out for him," Carlos warned. "That's what he does when he can't keep up. It's also why he spends so much time in the penalty box and why we're always playing short-handed."

Logan kept an eye out for Tyler for the rest of the scrimmage, but the game ended without further incident. By the end no one was bothering to keep track of the score.

As he exited the rink, Logan heard someone call his name and when he turned he saw a police officer standing just outside the locker room door.

The blood drained from Logan's face and his heart felt as though it had been seized in a viselike grip. The last time a policeman had shown up unexpectedly, it had been to tell him and his mom of his dad's accident.

As if sensing the boy's anxiousness, the officer, who looked to be in his late thirties, smiled and stuck out his hand.

"Hi, my name is Coach Brian Sweeney and I'm the coach of the Warriors' Pee Wee team."

Logan let out a sigh of relief and quickly slipped off his glove to shake hands.

"I heard we had a new hockey player in town, so I thought I'd stop by and check him out. You've got some skills, son," the coach said.

"Thanks," Logan replied.

"Where did you play last year?"

"Up in Winnipeg, for the Timberwolves. But my mom and I moved to West Bend, uh, recently ..."

"Well, maybe you've heard, we're looking for some good players. Our hockey organization is small, but we're growing. And we're always on the lookout for new talent. Based on what I just saw, I think you'd fit right in. Tryouts are Friday after school and then two hours on Saturday morning. Rosters will be posted on Sunday. Do you think you're interested?"

"Well, um, sure. I mean, I don't know," Logan stammered. "I'll have to ask my mom."

Logan shifted uncomfortably from one foot to the other and looked down at the ground as he spoke.

Coach Sweeney studied the boy in front of him, trying to read the conflicting emotions in his body language and voice.

"Of course, we're not the only game in town," he said, evenly. "There are other programs with better records than ours. And someone of your caliber might even have a shot at a triple A team."

"Right ... okay," Logan mumbled.

"Whatever you decide, you should probably check into it sooner rather than later. Most of the other teams are holding their tryouts this weekend too. And the top tier programs probably picked their teams last summer. But they might agree to give you a look, if you asked them."

"Got it," Logan said.

"Anyway," Coach Sweeney said, as he started to walk away, "we'll be here on Friday if you want to stop by."

After changing back into his sneakers and grabbing his skateboard, Logan stopped by the front desk on his way out where Joker was waiting patiently for him.

"Can I ask you a question?" he asked the guy behind the desk.

"Sure, you can ask, don't know if I'll have an answer though," the guy winked.

"How much does it cost to play hockey here?"

"It's not cheap, that's for sure. Somewhere around $3,000, I'd say. Maybe more."

Logan didn't know how much it had cost to play hockey in Canada, but he was pretty sure he and his mom couldn't afford the fees for the Warriors.

Chapter 4

Logan sat at the small desk in his bedroom, slowly turning the pages of the scrapbook. The book's brown leather cover was worn and slightly frayed at the edges. The yellowish light from the desk lamp cast a soft glow over the photographs and newspaper clippings inside.

He paused over one clipping, an article from the Winnipeg Gazette. The accompanying picture showed a group of players, their arms raised high in the air and wide grins of exuberant joy on their faces. The camera had caught that split second moment when the team knew for sure that victory was undeniable. In the center of the group was a tall, dark-haired man wearing number 27. Jon Michaud, Logan's father.

Logan ran his finger under the caption, "Jon Michaud, captain of the Manitoba Whalers, celebrates his team's victory over the Providence Ice Cats in the Calder Cup." The article described the thrilling 3 to 2 victory in the final game of the best of seven series. Michaud, the team's commanding center, was the top scorer in the series and had won MVP honors.

Logan's dad had been just 22 when the picture was taken. He'd spent years playing at the highest levels of junior hockey in Canada and then at the age of 20, he had been recruited by the Whalers to play in the American Hockey League, just one rung below the NHL.

On that glorious day, surrounded by his teammates and grinning into the camera, Jon Michaud's future had seemed so promising. But it was all an illusion. What his dad couldn't know was that just six months after that triumph, in tryout camp with the Buffalo Sabres, he would suffer a career-ending knee injury.

"It's so unfair," Logan muttered angrily as he slammed the book shut.

The harsh words broke the still silence of the room and Joker lifted his head up from the floor and quizzically cocked it to one side.

Logan flopped on the bed with his cellphone in one hand and ear buds in the other. He lay back on his pillow and let the sounds of the music from his phone's playlist sooth and distract him. He was still in that position an hour later when his mom shook his foot and told him to turn out the lights and go to sleep.

Logan slept fitfully that night and in his dreams a faceless enemy in a black jersey chased him around the rink. He turned and twisted and darted back and forth, yet the attacker kept gaining on him. Suddenly he was in the woods, running. But when he looked down, he saw that he was still wearing his skates. He heard a crash from behind and whirled around. Then he saw the blue uniform of a police officer . . . .

Logan sat bolt upright in bed, his heart pounding and his face covered by a thin sheen of perspiration. Joker stood up and came over to nuzzle his hand. He whimpered softly and went to the door with an expectant look on his face.

"You have to go out now? Really? What time is it?"

The digital clock on his nightstand read 3:13 a.m.

A three-quarter moon lent an eerie glow to the backyard. Joker scooted out the door and immediately headed for the trees at the far end of the yard. He quickly disappeared into their shadows.

"Joker!" Logan called out in a low voice. "What are you doing?"

Logan quietly closed the back door behind him and walked over to the spot where he had seen the dog enter the woods. He peered into their inky depths but couldn't see or hear anything except for the faint rustling of leaves.

"Joker!" he called again softly, this time more urgently.

As his eyes adjusted to the dim moonlight, Logan made his way carefully through the dense undergrowth. He finally spied Joker standing frozen at attention at the edge of the woods. His body was outlined by the lights from the industrial park on the other side of the street and he seemed to be watching something. When Logan reached him he grabbed the dog's collar and tried to pull him back towards the house, but Joker held firm.

"C'mon, buddy," Logan said. "Let's go."

Suddenly the bright gleam of headlights appeared at the far end of the street as a car turned the corner, and both Logan and Joker instinctively slipped back into the darkness of the woods.

As they watched, a yellow sports car turned into the driveway of Exotic Auto Repair and came to a stop outside the fence. It flashed its lights on and off and immediately the heavy chain-link fence began to slide open with a rattling sound. The car moved forward and a man stepped out of the building's side door to greet the driver.

Logan looked down in surprise when he heard Joker growl low in his throat. When he looked back up he saw the man from the building hand the driver what appeared to be a small bundle. Logan could see elaborate tattoos covering the driver's forearms and neck in the light of the car's open door. With his flat bill cap and sagging jeans the guy looked like a street thug from one of those cop shows Logan occasionally watched.

Within seconds another car turned the corner and slowly glided to a stop by the curb. The driver hopped in and the second car took off.

Meanwhile the guy from Exotic Auto had opened a garage door and was maneuvering the sports car inside. The chain-link fence rattled shut and Logan watched as the garage door descended and the sports car disappeared from sight.

The street grew quiet again.

"C'mon," Logan said to Joker, tugging on his collar.

This time Joker followed him willingly.

Chapter 5

Logan spent the next couple of days avoiding the other hockey players at school. He kept his head down in the hallways between periods and hid out in the library during lunch. Finally Ryan and Tyler cornered him at his locker.

"Hey," Ryan said. "Are you coming to tryouts after school today?"

Logan placed his math book on the top shelf and slammed the locker door shut.

"Um, uh, no," Logan said, haltingly. "I can't make it."

"Can't or won't?" Tyler asked.

Unable to meet the other boys' eyes, Logan simply looked down at the ground and shook his head.

"Yeah, that's what I thought," Tyler sneered. "We're not good enough for you."

Logan quickly looked up. "No, that's not it. It's just..." but he couldn't finish and his words trailed off.

After an awkward moment of silence, Ryan elbowed Tyler. "Whatever," he said to Logan. "Let's go, Ty."

Staring down the hallway at their retreating backs, Logan wondered if his life could get any worse.

That weekend Logan stayed close to home. When he wasn't downloading songs from the computer, he was sprawled on the sofa in the family room playing video games. Boredom soon set in. There were only so many ways one could kill a bloodthirsty zombie. He had already rescued all the survivors on Zombie Island and used all the weapons in his arsenal in the process. Now he was simply spinning around in circles picking off defenseless targets.

He groaned when his mom suggested he get a start on his homework. But as the endless Saturday wore on, he finally pulled a paperback book from his backpack and started reading. Anything to distract himself from thoughts of the tryouts that were taking place at the ice rink.

On Sunday his mom announced that his grandparents had invited them over for a barbeque. Grandpa Frank and Nona lived on the east side of town in a large, white brick house with a front walk bordered by red geraniums. The houses on that side of town were grander than the ones in his neighborhood and most had spacious lawns shaded by graceful old oak trees.

"Well, come on in," his grandmother said, greeting them at the front door as she took the plate of brownies his mother had prepared from Logan's hands. "Why, I think you've grown another inch, Logan," she teased.

It was a standing joke in their family. Not a week went by that one of his grandparents failed to mention how tall he was for his age or how much he'd grown since they'd last seen him. Probably because everyone on his mom's side of the family was below average in height, except his mom, whom they sometimes kidded must have been switched at the hospital.

"Joker can stay outside if you like," Logan said.

Joker looked up at the adults with a sad, mournful expression in his brown eyes.

"Nonsense," his grandmother said. "Of course he can come in."

"Good work, buddy," Logan whispered. "Now just don't knock anything over."

The interior of the house was elegant with its dark wood furniture, crystal chandeliers and oriental rugs on the floors. The sunny kitchen at the back of the house opened onto a screened porch, and Logan could smell the smoke from the grill the minute he stepped out back.

"Maybe another couple of minutes and I can start the vegetables," his grandfather called out. He was using tongs to spread the greyish charcoal lumps evenly on the bottom of the kettle grill. No propane tanks for Grandpa Frank, he only used charcoal. Once Logan had made the mistake of asking why and was rewarded for his curiosity with a 30-minute lecture on the inferiority of gas grills and the flavorless meat they produced. *Why you might as well cook your steak in the oven," his grandfather had said.*

"How's school going?" Grandpa Frank asked after Logan wandered over to stand next to him.

"It's going," Logan replied.

Grandpa Frank began to layer red peppers, zucchini and onions on the outer edge of the grill's surface.

"I remember when your mom and your Aunt Lily were going to that school. They had just built it and everything there was brand spanking new. 'State of the art,' the principal kept saying. 'This school is state of the art!'"

"Yeah, it's probably not state of the art anymore," Logan admitted. "But they do have these cool white board things that teachers hook up to their computers. They're like giant computer screens at the front of the room. You can surf the web on them and research stuff."

"I can't keep up with all the new technology," Grandpa Frank said, shaking his head. "Your grandmother just bought one of those smart tablets that you download books on. She was reading something on it last night."

The sound and smell of the sizzling steaks drew Joker over to the grill. Logan's grandmother brought out a bowl of potato salad and some rolls and placed them on the table in the screened porch.

"I don't know," his grandfather continued. "There's something about the touch and feel of a real book that's comforting to me. I guess I just like the sound of pages turning."

He turned to Logan with a wry smile. "Besides what would I do with all those books in my library?"

Logan's grandfather had practiced law in West Bend for almost 40 years. He was basically semi-retired now but still rented office space and saw clients two or three days a week. His library at home was wall-to-wall books with everything from leather bound legal books to classics like *The Adventures of Huckleberry Finn* and *To Kill a Mockingbird*. The room had a quiet, dignified air and when Logan was little he thought he had to whisper when he went in there, just like a real library.

Dinner was a relaxed affair out on the back porch. The late afternoon sun was warm and the porch overlooked a backyard still in full bloom with bright pink and yellow flowers. Afterwards as his mom and grandparents sat around the table drinking coffee, Logan strapped on his rollerblades and headed up the street with Joker to a small park.

His skates glided smoothly over the even asphalt pavement. Suddenly Joker raced on ahead. There was someone kicking a ball in the grassy field and the dog, thinking it was a game, pounced on the ball and butted it with his head into the street.

"Hey!" a voice yelled. "Stop that!"

As Logan skidded to a stop, he saw Megan Sweeney running towards him.

Chapter 6

Logan quickly scooped up the soccer ball and handed it to Megan.

"Sorry about that," he apologized.

Meanwhile Joker had stopped at the sidewalk and was wagging his tail, hoping for some more fun.

"That's okay," Megan said with a rueful smile. "He's pretty fast. We could probably use him on our team."

Joker barked once to get their attention and Megan dropped the ball and kicked it back into the field. The dog sprinted after it.

"So, um, have you got your classes figured out yet?" Megan asked after an uncomfortable pause. "I mean, I saw you taking tests during lunch period."

"Yeah, not quite. I'm still waiting for my results."

"Oh, right," Megan said. She looked over her shoulder at Joker who was now busily sniffing the shrubs and grass in the park.

After another awkward pause, Logan asked, "Are you trying out for the soccer team?"

"No, I'm already on it. I'm just practicing."

Logan nodded his head and shifted slightly on his skates.

"What are you doing here?" Megan finally asked.

"What are *you* doing here?" Logan answered.

"I live here – in that yellow house over there."

Logan's eyes followed the direction of her finger and he realized she was pointing to the house directly across the street from his grandparents'.

"Oh," Logan said.

"So what are *you* doing here," Megan asked again.

"Visiting my grandparents. They live in the white house across the street from yours."

"Your grandparents are the Schneiders?" she asked.

"Yup."

"Oh," Megan nodded thoughtfully. "They've lived here for years."

"Yeah, my mom grew up here. She even went to West Bend High."

Megan gave Logan a quizzical look and opened her mouth as if to say something but then seemed to change her mind.

She glanced away before changing the subject. "So how come you're not at the ice rink? Ryan said the team had a meeting today."

"Yeah, well ... I'm not on the team."

"Really? Why not?" Megan looked surprised. "Ryan said you were, like, the best one out there."

Now it was Logan's turn to open his mouth and then abruptly clamp it shut, as if to bite back the words on the tip of his tongue.

He shook his head instead and sighed.

"I, uh, have a bunch of stuff going on, and I don't know ... maybe next year," he ended lamely.

Despite his nonchalant words, Logan couldn't hide the look of misery on his face. Megan watched him quietly.

Joker suddenly ran over as if on cue and playfully nudged Logan's leg. The dog's appearance broke the tension and Logan reached down to scratch his head.

Megan smiled, "What's his name?"

"Joker"

"Like the bad guy from the Batman movie?"

"Actually he's Joker the Second. He was named after a dog my dad had when he was little," Logan said.

"I'm serious about the offer to join the soccer team. We could use his speed. Last year we only won two games."

Logan smiled faintly, "He'll think about it. Right, Joker?"

Joker barked twice in response.

"Well, I should probably get going," Logan said. "See you around school."

"Yeah, see ya," Megan replied, and as Logan pushed off and headed back up the street towards his grandparents' house, Megan stared at his back with an intent look on her face.

Logan was moved into the honors math class on Monday. Megan Sweeney looked up when he walked in late with his note from the registrar's office and smiled in acknowledgement. He slipped into a desk two rows behind hers next to the windows.

Meanwhile he kept his distance from the other hockey players. It wasn't really that difficult. The school was fairly large and the only one in any of his classes was Dylan, who sat in the back of his science class. When the final bell of the day rang, Logan grabbed his skateboard and took off before any of the kids standing in the bus lines had even boarded their buses.

On Friday, the entire Pee Wee team wore matching black Warriors t-shirts. Logan was sitting in a cubicle in the far corner of the library at lunchtime, hidden by a large stack of books, when he heard the familiar voices of Ryan and Tyler not more than six feet away.

Chapter 7

They were wandering the aisles looking for a book.

"How do you spell the author's name?" Ryan asked.

"B - L - E - V - E - N - S," said Tyler.

"Okay, we're in the right spot. It should be here."

There was a brief silence and then the sounds of footsteps and a third voice.

"Hey, Ryan."

"Hey, Matt."

"What time is the game tomorrow?" Matt asked.

"1:30," said Ryan.

"Are you guys pumped?"

"You bet!" Tyler answered, a confident tone in his voice. "This year it's gonna be different. This year the Bears are gonna get their butts kicked all over the ice."

"Yeah?"

"Yeah, we've been working out all summer, skating and doing off-ice stuff, building up our endurance," continued Tyler. "Trust me, we're ready for them."

"It'll be a tough game for sure," Ryan said a little more cautiously. "But I think we've got a good shot."

"Well, good luck," Matt said.

Logan heard Matt move off, and then Tyler exclaimed, "Here it is. *The Battle of Antietam: A Turning Point in the Civil War* by Richard Blevens."

"You know, Ty, I'm not sure I'd go around telling everyone this game is a slam dunk."

"Why not? What's wrong with a little trash talk? It builds confidence. Besides, who knows, maybe some of it will filter back to the Bears."

"Somehow I don't think the team that's been number one for the last three years and has only lost 2 games is quaking in their skates."

"Well, they should be," Tyler said angrily. "We worked hard over the summer. Coach Brian came up with some sweet plays and we practiced four times a week. What about all those drills? Plus we're bigger and stronger."

"Everyone is bigger and stronger. I'm sure the Bears grew over the summer too."

"I don't care," Tyler said. "While everyone else was out playing baseball, we were focusing on hockey. I think it'll pay off."

There was a slight pause and then Tyler asked, "What's wrong? Why are you suddenly doubting everything?"

Ryan sighed, "I don't know. I was feeling great about the team and then some guy shows up to Rat Ice and blows everyone away. What if he tried out for the Bears?"

"Forget about him," Tyler said. "He's nothing, just a fancy skater. One check and he goes right into the boards."

"That wasn't a check, it was a hook and you blindsided him. That doesn't count."

"Whatever. I doubt he went to the Bears. Their rink is, like, forty minutes away and that's pretty far to go for practices. If anything he went to the Huskies," Tyler added. "Their rink is much closer."

"*Great*," Ryan said in a sarcastic voice. "That makes me feel *much* better. The Huskies were only the second best team in the division last year."

"Look, Ryan. I know these teams are good and they have a lot of solid players. But we have something they don't have – toughness. If we can start being more physical out there on the ice, I know we can beat these guys."

"That's fine if you're a defensive player, but hitting guys doesn't put the puck in the net. We need players who can score, and the one thing that Logan guy could do was score goals."

"You can score goals too, Ryan," Tyler said encouragingly. "And if our defense is solid, you won't have to score that many – just a couple to win the game."

"Maybe," Ryan said, not sounding thoroughly convinced.

"Trust me," said Tyler. "When have I ever been wrong?"

Logan could hear Ryan's snort of laughter as the two boys moved out of earshot.

In his sixth period gym class, Logan overheard some other boys talking about the big game on Saturday. Putting bits and pieces of conversation together, he learned that the Bears were considered the best hockey team in the northern region of the state. Three key players anchored the team, a tough goalie who rarely let any pucks get past him and two brothers who were big, strong and fast. One brother played offense and the other played defense and their father was the team's head coach. Last year the team's record was 18 wins and no losses.

Later that night Logan sat at the computer desk in the family room and surfed the Internet looking for information on the local hockey teams. He pulled up the website for the Northern Suburban Hockey League and checked the statistics for last year. The Bears had definitely ended the season at the top spot, but the Huskies weren't far behind with a 15 and 3 record. The West Bend Warriors were second from the bottom with only 4 wins and 14 losses.

He also looked up the individual player stats. The leading scorer was someone from the Bears named Luke Frankel with 38 goals and 14 assists, for a total of 52 points. Next on the list was a player from the Huskies with 29 points and then someone from the Panthers. The top scorer for the Warriors, Ryan Sweeney, was somewhere in the middle of the pack with only 7 goals and 3 assists.

Even more impressive, the Bears' goalie had allowed only 9 goals all season. Fully two-thirds of the team's victories had been shutouts.

The Warriors were on top in one category though. Penalty minutes. Tyler Grayson led everyone in the league with 63 penalty minutes, including one 10 minute major for a game misconduct.

Logan powered down the computer and stared at the blank screen. He desperately wanted to play in the game tomorrow. Just hearing about the dominance of the Bears and their impenetrable goalie stirred his competitive spirit and made him long to get out there on the ice. He knew he could bring some offensive firepower to the Warriors. He just knew it.

The next morning Logan helped his mom do some chores around the house. He picked up the dirty clothes in his room and unpacked a couple of boxes in the garage that had been lying around since the move from Canada. When she left at noon to run some errands, he tried unsuccessfully to distract himself with video games and music. But thoughts of the game kept intruding. He wondered just how good this supposedly invincible team really was. Finally curiosity won out and Logan decided to head over to the ice rink to see if he could figure out a way to slip into the building without being seen. He didn't need to stay for the whole game. He just wanted to catch a few minutes of the mighty Bears in action.

Chapter 8

Logan locked Joker in the house and pulled a baseball cap low over his eyes. Grabbing his skateboard, he again took a shortcut through the woods behind his house. As he emerged onto the sidewalk he noticed that the auto repair shop across the street was dark and deserted looking. Despite the fact it was a sunny Saturday afternoon and most of the neighboring businesses were open, there were no signs of life at Exotic Auto and the chain link fence surrounding the yard was tightly shut.

In contrast the area around the ice rink was a beehive of activity. As Logan approached, he saw the parking lot was full of cars and, judging by the number of Bears decals on the rear windows, it seemed that quite a few Bears fans had shown up for the game.

When he noticed a side door had been propped open with a brick, he quickly slipped through it.

The door opened onto a short hallway. To his left was a metal staircase that led to a small second floor loft overlooking the rink. Logan went and stood behind a pillar directly above center ice. There were a few younger kids running around the open loft space, slapping at a rubber ball with their hockey sticks, but they ignored Logan. He didn't recognize anyone he knew.

The stands below were jam-packed. The skaters had already begun their warm-ups and were taking practice shots at their own goals. The Warriors looked sharp in their black and white jerseys with cobalt blue lettering. Each jersey had a large "W" on the front and the skater's last name and number stenciled on the back. The Bears were in orange and black with the logo of a bear's head on the front of their jerseys.

Finally a buzzer sounded the end of the pregame warm-up and both teams skated over to their benches for some final words of advice from the coaches. As the Warriors huddled around Coach Sweeney, Logan saw Tyler Grayson with his back to the bleachers, wearing number 19. Ryan Sweeney was standing next to him with number 7 on his jersey.

The head referee signaled to start the game and the first lines skated out to center ice. Logan noted as the two centers faced off against each other that the Bears' center was nearly a head taller than Carlos Fuentes, his counterpart on the Warriors. Logan wondered if he was one-half of the formidable brother pair who was currently dominating the league. He didn't have long to wait for his answer.

Fweeet! The referee dropped the puck and Carlos was quickly knocked off balance as the Bears' center hooked the black rubber disk and slapped it sideways to his left wing. The wingman dropped backed slightly and then angled a precision pass right back to his teammate who had already streaked past Carlos and was now just outside the blue line. Dodging one Warriors defenseman, he fired a hard shot at the goal that was deflected at the very last second by the Warriors' goalie, Brad Lyman. Brad moved swiftly to block the left corner of the net as skaters battled for control of the puck behind him.

A Bear wrestled possession away from the Warriors defenders and shot the puck out to one of his defensemen who had crept forward. Meanwhile the Bears' center had circled back and was using his body to obstruct the goalie's view. The next shot bounded off the goalie's pads and skittered to a stop right in front of the net. Almost casually, the big center swung around and tapped it in. As the player raised his arms in triumph, Logan saw the name on the back of his jersey. L. Frankel.

Cheers erupted from the stands and Logan glanced over at the scoreboard clock. It had taken only 25 seconds for the Bears to score. They had made it look almost too easy.

As the first lines returned to the bench, the number two lines skated out to square off. This time, the two centers were more evenly matched in height and it was the Warriors player who won the face-off. He dumped the puck behind him and the defenseman who picked it up dropped back while the three forwards spread out. Then the defensive player slowly skated forward, moving the puck from side to side, daring the other team to try and steal it from him.

When a Bear finally charged him, he made a quick pass to James, the other defenseman, who then passed the puck up along the right boards.

With the puck in Bears territory, the Warriors did a nice job of controlling the play. The center swung around behind the net but couldn't get a shot off so he passed the puck over to his wing, who in turn dumped it off to James at the point. James wound up and took a huge slap shot that hit the goalie's kneepads and bounced away. A Warriors player was right there to pick up the rebound but the lightning fast glove of the goalie blocked the shot.

Whoa! Against almost any other goalie that would have been a goal, Logan thought. No wonder this team hasn't lost any games.

As the first period wore on, Logan began to realize a few things. First, with the exception of the number one lines, the teams were really quite evenly matched. When the second and third lines went up against each other, neither side dominated and the game turned into a real contest. The problem was that after the Warriors had come close to scoring a couple of times, the Bears' coach began inserting his star center into every other shift and lessening the playing time of some of the other players. When the big guy was on the ice, his aggressive play changed the dynamics of the game.

Second, the goalie for the Bears was first rate. His reflexes were unbelievably quick and he had great peripheral vision, able to sense when an opponent was hanging off to the side ready to poach a rebound. And if someone got a rebound shot off, he was right there with the save. He didn't seem to have any weaknesses that Logan could see.

By the end of the first period, the score was 3 to 0 in favor of the Bears. The Warriors had hung tough after the initial quick goal by the Bears, but once the opposing coach started putting in only his best players, the Warriors were outmatched.

Right before the buzzer sounded the end of the period, one of the Bears' defenders slammed Ryan into the boards and the referee blew his whistle. Tyler charged over and started jabbing his finger in the opposing player's face and yelling at him. He looked ready to take a swing at someone and might have if a couple of his teammates hadn't intervened and pulled him off the ice. Logan watched as Tyler threw his stick and gloves on the bench in frustration.

Uh oh, Logan thought. I have a bad feeling about this.

Chapter 9

The second period started with a Bears player sitting in the penalty box, serving a two minute penalty for boarding. That gave the Warriors a 5 to 4 player advantage on the power play. Ryan was now in the center spot in place of Carlos who had been ineffective on face-offs against the much larger Frankel.

Ryan hunched over to receive the puck drop, his gloves positioned low on his stick. Even from his faraway perch in the loft, Logan could see the tenseness in Ryan's body. He looked like a coiled spring ready to explode.

The rubber disk hit the ice and the two centers slashed ferociously at it with their sticks. The puck ricocheted to Dylan who held it momentarily and then sent it back to one of the Warriors defensemen.

Meanwhile the four Bears skaters formed a protective shield around their goalie. One of the Bears lunged forward to challenge the puck handler but dropped back after he passed it off to another player along the boards. The whole point was to be aggressive but not let the other team creep in too close to the net.

Although the Warriors did a good job of moving the puck around, the Bears were nimble skaters and did not allow their opponents many opportunities to penetrate the defense. Shifting deftly from side to side, they quickly closed off any openings that materialized. At one point, after a battle for possession in the corner, a Bear emerged with the puck on his stick and sent it the length of the ice. A Warriors defenseman quickly retrieved it but precious seconds were ticking away on the penalty clock.

Logan could see that both Frankel brothers were out on the ice. The one playing defense was every bit as aggressive as his brother. Then one of the Warriors slapped a hard pass to the point and it jumped off Tyler's stick. Luke Frankel chose that exact moment to attack and was able to get the end of his stick on the puck and flick it away. Using his forward momentum and long strides, he reached the puck first and, grabbing it, stormed down the ice. The nearest Warrior was a half-length behind.

Brad squared himself in the center of the net. Frankel dodged left, then right and at the last possible second lifted a shot over the goalie's far shoulder. *Score!*

The Bears drummed their sticks against the boards in celebration. Logan saw Tyler angrily slam his stick to the ground. It was humiliating to have the puck stolen away like that but doubly humiliating to be scored upon when the other team was short-handed. Luke Frankel skated to the bench to receive congratulatory glove taps from his teammates and then raised his arms in triumph before skating back to center ice.

A little too much public celebrating, Logan thought. Tyler's not gonna like that. He's pissed enough as it is.

The same lines returned to face off again and this time Ryan was knocked off-balance as the puck shot sideways to one of the Bears. The defenseman backed up and stickhandled to kill time on the penalty clock before passing off to another Bear who then shoveled the puck forward along the boards.

Both Frankel and Tyler went after the loose puck. Frankel reached it first and seconds later Tyler crashed into him at full speed, his stick held firmly in both hands. The force of the impact sent Frankel sprawling to the ground and he lay there motionless for a few moments. The referee blew his whistle but before he could reach the players, Luke Frankel's brother, Drew, shoved Tyler against the boards and Tyler responded by swinging his fist at Drew's helmet. The two were soon down on the ice, locked in a wrestling hold. With their bulky gloves and thick padding, they couldn't do much damage but the referee and a couple of teammates quickly pulled them apart.

Luke Frankel got slowly to his feet and made his way back to the bench as the crowd applauded solemnly. The game was halted while the referees conferred with the scorekeeper and both coaches about penalties. Finally both Tyler and Drew Frankel skated over to the penalty boxes. Tyler received a two-minute penalty for cross-checking and both boys were given five-minute majors for fighting. Another Warrior was sent to the box to serve out Tyler's minor penalty.

Play resumed and for the next 45 seconds the teams were evenly matched with four skaters apiece. Then the Bears' boarding penalty expired and they were back at full strength. It took them less than a minute to score again and this time neither Frankel brother was on the ice. The score was now 5 to 0.

When Luke Frankel returned to the game, after sitting out a couple of shifts, he was not the dominant force he had been earlier. Nevertheless, the Bears managed to score twice more, and by the end of the second period, the home team was down by seven goals.

At the sound of the buzzer, both teams trouped back to the locker rooms. Meanwhile a machine that looked something like a giant riding lawnmower came out to resurface the ice. Chugging along at a snail's pace, it moved back and forth in even, overlapping lines leaving a fresh surface of ice in its wake. The younger kids resumed their game of floor hockey in the loft area and again they ignored Logan's presence.

The teams returned to the ice after 15 minutes and began warming up. As the third period got underway, Logan noticed a change in the Warriors' strategy. Everyone, with the exception of Tyler, seemed to have adopted a tentative, more defensive style of play. They were now playing dump and chase. Whenever the forwards got ahold of the puck they quickly dumped it in the offensive zone and then chased it into the corners.

The time on the clock wound down as the two teams skated back and forth the length of the ice, trading possession of the puck. Finally a Bear made a shot on goal and the rebound jumped off Brad's kneepad. The goalie quickly slapped his glove on the ice to cover it at the same time that another Bears player, who had been hanging off to the side, tried to poke it into the net with his stick. Before the referee could whistle the puck dead, Tyler got in front of Brad and shoved his opponent away from the goal post. The other kid shoved back and within seconds the referees were pulling the two skaters apart.

Chapter 10

Tyler was given a game misconduct for his second fighting offense and sent to the locker room. Logan watched a few more minutes of the game before slipping out the back door unseen. He glided home on his skateboard lost in thought. For about the fiftieth time that week he bitterly railed against the unfairness of it all. He should have been out there.

On Monday the hockey team seemed subdued and there was little talk at school about the disastrous outing against the Bears. The Warriors played a Tuesday night game against a bottom tier team and lost 4 to 1. Tyler had been given a one game suspension, and he served it watching from the stands with the parents and other students since league rules prohibited him from sitting on the bench with his teammates.

"Are you sure you want to get a job now, bud?" his mom asked, as she poured him a glass of orange juice. "Why not wait until summer?"

Logan munched on a slice of toast under Joker's watchful gaze, the dog's expressive eyes silently begging.

"Here, boy," he said, slipping him a piece of the crust. "The problem with that is everyone will be looking for a job for the summer. I figure if I start now, I'll get the jump on everybody else."

"What about your school work? I don't want that to suffer and you really haven't given yourself time to adjust to the new school."

"It's only four or five hours a week and Mr. Perelli said I could pretty much set my own schedule. He said just to let him know if I had, like, a test or something due, and he'd work around it."

"That's awfully nice of him," his mom said.

"He knows Grandpa Frank and Nona, and his kids used to play hockey. And I guess he knew Dad – or at least knew who he was," Logan added quietly.

Landing the job at Perelli's Food Market was the one stroke of luck Logan had had recently. Perelli's Market was located on a well-lit street not far from his house, and he could easily rollerblade there and back after school or on the weekends. Logan had never applied anywhere for a job before, but he had stopped by the store on Monday after school and asked to speak to the person hiring who turned out to be Mr. Perelli himself. As he told his mom, Mr. Perelli was a big hockey fan – both his sons had played the sport up through high school and he himself had played when he was younger. They had talked for quite a while. Mr. Perelli had said he needed someone to unpack boxes and stock shelves and his only requirement was that Logan clear things with his mom first.

"Besides, you don't want me spending all my free time playing video games, do you?" Logan asked with a sly grin.

"Alright, but if your grades start slipping, I'll have to reconsider my decision."

"Thanks, Mom."

Logan arrived at Perelli's Market promptly at 4:00 o'clock. The assistant produce manager, a lanky high school kid named Mike, showed him where to stash his rollerblades and jacket and gave him a long, green apron to put on. Boxes of red and green apples were stacked high in a corner of the back storage room and Mike showed Logan how to open them using a metal crowbar. Then they lifted a couple of the boxes onto a rolling cart and wheeled the cart out onto the produce floor.

"It's simple, really," Mike said. "Just move the old stuff down closer to the front where people can get to it more easily and put the new stuff up on top. Line everything up in rows, and if you come across a spoiled piece of fruit, just toss it in this empty box."

"Right."

"Oh, and be sure to put the apples in the right spot. I know they all look the same, but we sell about twenty different varieties of apples here, everything from Macintoshes to Jonagolds. Each one has a sticker with its name on it, so just match the sticker to the sign below and you'll be fine."

"Got it," Logan said.

As Mike walked off, Logan started moving the apples around and making room for the new product. An hour flew by and Logan was working so intently on a display of Bosch pears that he failed to notice the boys in the store until they were almost on top of him.

They were over by the candy aisle where the store had a colorful display of bulk candy lined up in glass jars. He could see Tyler dipping a metal scoop into a jar of gummy worms and shoveling them into a clear plastic bag. Standing next to Tyler were Ryan and Dylan. None of the boys had noticed him yet, so Logan slipped behind a large pillar and turned his face away. But they were speaking loud enough that he could still hear snatches of their conversation.

They were talking about a tournament in Indiana that was scheduled for the upcoming weekend. The team had rented a bus to travel there and back and the players were staying in a hotel with a heated indoor pool and a game room. If they had time the weather cooperated, they might even get to visit a local go-kart track. Ryan had just bought a new stick because his old one had snapped in the last game and he was excited to try it out. Most of the team was planning to leave school early on Friday.

Logan slowly started pushing the cart towards the back room, careful to keep his back to the group, when the conversation suddenly stopped and he knew he'd been found out.

"Hey, well, will you look at who it is." Logan was sure he could recognize Tyler's sneering voice anywhere.

He turned around and saw all three boys staring at him.

"I'm surprised you even have time for a job, what with school and trying out for the Olympic team and all."

Dylan made a strangled sound in his throat that sounded a bit like a laugh he was trying to suppress. Ryan just looked at the ground, but Logan thought he saw a slight smile playing on his lips.

Logan bit back a mean retort on the tip of his tongue about the team's disastrous game against the Bears and nodded his head toward Tyler instead.

"I think you're supposed to eat the candy *after* you pay for it."

Tyler stared back at Logan, a defiant look on his face and a green worm dangling from the corner of his mouth. Then Logan turned away and headed for the storage room.

I kept my cool, Mom, he thought. You'd be proud of me.

Chapter 11

It was becoming something of a ritual for Logan and his mom to spend Sundays at his grandparents' house. Logan didn't mind, really, because it was the one night of the week he knew he'd get a delicious home-cooked meal. With his mom working late and then fighting traffic to get home, they often had fast food or leftovers a couple times a week.

Tonight Grandpa Frank was taking a break from the grill and they were having fried chicken, mashed potatoes and gravy, and corn on the cob. Nona said it was late in the season for corn, but she had found some fresh-looking produce over at Perelli's Market.

"I hear you're working for Sam Perelli now, Logan," Grandpa Frank said. "I remember watching his two sons play for West Bend's Varsity hockey team.

Those boys were good athletes. They played lacrosse too, I think."

"Don't you think Logan is a little young to have a job, Anne?" Nona asked, casting a worried look at Logan's mom.

"Of course not," Grandpa Frank said, interrupting. "I had a job when I was his age. I remember mowing lawns in the summer and shoveling driveways in the winter. It was hard work but I was happy to have money in my pocket."

Nona rolled her eyes and smiled. "That was fifty years ago, Frank. Times have changed. Most young boys today are so busy with all their different activities and sports they don't have time for much else. Everything is so organized, so overscheduled."

Then she turned to Logan, "Besides, what about the hockey team? When do your practices start?"

Logan shot his mom a quick glance, "I'm not playing hockey this year. Maybe next year."

"But why not?" Grandpa Frank asked, his face a mixture of surprise and concern. "You love the sport and you're a terrific skater. Just like your dad."

There was an awkward silence and then his mom spoke up, "We just thought that with a new school and a new town, it might be best to wait a bit and get settled in before he jumped into something."

"But that's the point," Nona protested. "Because Logan is new, joining a team is the best way to make new friends and settle into a new environment. When are the tryouts?"

"They were two weeks ago," Logan said quietly.

Nona blinked and then shifted her gaze from Logan to his mom and then back to Logan. Finally she said, "Logan, why don't you take Joker up the street to the park for some exercise while we older folks have another cup of coffee?"

Feeling the tension in the air, Logan was more than happy to oblige and grabbed a freshly baked chocolate chip cookie from the counter on his way out the door.

Because Logan was on foot instead of his usual rollerblades, Joker streaked ahead and was soon out of view. By the time Logan caught up with him, the dog was circling a clump of bushes, his nose to the ground, trying to pick up the scents of other animals.

Logan sat down on one of the red plastic swings and rocked back and forth. He gazed out at the open grassy area of the park with his back to the street and didn't hear the other boy come up behind him until he was only a few yards away. When Logan turned around the surprise on his face mirrored the equal surprise on Ryan's.

"Oh, I didn't realize it was you," Ryan said stiffly.

"Yeah, I was over at my grandparents' house for dinner," Logan said. Seeing the look of confusion on Ryan's face, he added, "They live across the street from you."

At the sound of another voice, Joker's ears perked up and he trotted over to stand next to Logan.

"And this is my dog, Joker."

"Hey, Joker," Ryan gave the dog a friendly smile and extended his hand. Joker ambled over, his tail wagging.

"So, how do you know I live across the street from your grandparents?"

"I ran into your sister here once, a couple of weeks ago. She was kicking around a soccer ball."

Ryan nodded his head slowly.

Finally, Logan said, "So where's your soccer ball?"

"What?"

"I mean, why are you here at the park? To swing on the swings? Play on the monkey bars?"

Ryan ignored the sarcastic undertone. "I'm here to run a few laps. Just trying to build up my endurance."

"Four times around the park is about a mile," he added.

After another uncomfortable pause Logan asked, "So how'd you guys do in the tournament?"

"We tied one and lost three."

Logan didn't know what to say so he just stared at the ground. Finally, Ryan started to move off, "Well, maybe I should get started."

He walked about ten feet and then whirled around.

"I know Tyler can be a jerk sometimes, but I don't understand why you even bothered to show up for Rat Ice that one time. I mean, you obviously had no

70

intention of trying out for the team. Was it just to prove to how much better you were than the rest of us? To show us we were nothing more than a bunch of guys playing for some lousy local team who were no match for a real Canadian hockey player?"

Logan glared back at Ryan and all the pent up frustration of the last few weeks boiled to the surface.

"You know what, Ryan? You're clueless, just totally clueless. You have no idea how lucky you are, how easy you have it. You want to play hockey? Sure, your parents will sign you right up. Write a big fat check and you're on the team. Need a new stick because your old one broke? No problem, Mommy and Daddy will buy you a new one, top of the line, whatever you want. A trip to Indiana, staying overnight in a hotel, team dinners in a restaurant? All that costs money but you don't have to worry because your parents can afford it. No big deal. Well, the truth is not everyone has thousands dollars to splurge on some sport for their kid. Not everyone can afford to pay the kind of money it takes to play hockey. And not every kid can sit back like you and not worry about where the money will come from. Some of us have to go out and find jobs and help pay for it ourselves."

As Logan spat out the last sentence, he jumped up from the swing and turned on his heel. Then he strode off without a backwards glance.

Chapter 12

The next morning Logan told his mom that his stomach hurt and he didn't feel well enough to go to school. She gave him a puzzled look but said nothing and agreed to call the attendance office.

"I'll check on you around noon," she promised. "There's some chicken noodle soup in the pantry that you can heat up in the microwave if you get hungry."

The day dragged on endlessly and Logan soon tired of his video games and music. He was dozing on the sofa when a knock on the door startled him awake.

Standing on the front steps was Ryan Sweeney.

"What do you want?" Logan asked, in a decidedly unfriendly tone.

"You weren't in school today so I thought I'd stop by. I wanted to talk to you."

"How'd you find out where I live?"

"Megan got your address from the front office. Oh, here's your math homework by the way. She told them she would drop it off."

Logan stared at the sheets of paper in Ryan's outstretched hand.

"Hi, Joker," Ryan said. The dog came up behind Logan and started wagging his tail in greeting.

Traitor dog, Logan thought.

Logan grabbed the math papers and stepped aside to let Ryan enter. He then led the way into the family room. Eyeing the rumpled blanket and pillow on the sofa, Ryan nodded and said, "I guess you're sick, huh?"

"Something like that."

"Yeah, well like I said, I wanted to talk to you after, um, yesterday at the park," Ryan looked over at Logan who was staring stonily at the wall.

"Look," Ryan rushed on. "I was definitely out of line with that crack about you thinking you're better than us. I mean, I don't even know you or anything about you . . . at least I didn't yesterday anyway."

This last statement caused Logan to glance up sharply and then quickly avert his eyes again.

"I can't imagine what it would be like to move to a new town, a new country even," Ryan went on. "I've lived in West Bend my whole life and, well, it must be tough for you and your mom . . . starting over and all."

Logan swallowed the lump in his throat and found he couldn't speak.

Ryan sighed and sat down on a chair. Joker came over and put his chin on Ryan's knee while Ryan stroked his head. "Hey, your dog really likes me. That must count for something."

"He's a dog."

"An obviously *intelligent* dog," Ryan countered with a grin.

"No, an obviously *bored* dog who's been stuck in the house with me all day."

Finally Logan sat down too and said in a tired voice, "Believe me, I don't for a second think that I'm too good to play for your team. But at the moment, it's just not possible."

"Because it costs too much money?"

Logan's nod was almost imperceptible.

"But you played in Canada, right?"

"Yeah, but in Canada, hockey is a lot cheaper. It costs maybe $300 a year to play on a team. Every town has a rink and everybody skates. People skate outside in the fall and winter too."

"Is it that much more here?"

"It's probably ten times that amount here. Thousands of dollars. And then there's the cost of equipment, uniforms and traveling to out-of-town tournaments. It really adds up."

"I had no idea," Ryan said quietly.

"Yeah I didn't either, until recently. But a lot of stuff has happened this past year and I . . ." Logan's voice trailed off and he didn't finish his sentence.

After a slight pause, Ryan said, "My mom told me your dad was a great hockey player. She said he almost made it to the NHL."

"Almost." Then Logan added, "He tore up his knee in tryout camp and had to quit. So how does your mom know about my dad?"

"My parents have been friends with your grandparents for years. Plus, it's a small town."

Logan nodded. "My mom grew up in West Bend. That's why we moved back here in the first place."

He looked around the room.

"You know, I don't mind it here. I really don't. We moved around a lot in Canada so I guess I'm used to being the new guy anyway. But I really miss playing hockey. It's the one thing I can do."

"Maybe you could keep coming to Rat Ice."

"I don't know," Logan said. "Everyone would wonder why I'm not on the team . . . I don't wanna have to answer any questions. I think I'll just keep saving my money and hopefully try out next year."

"The problem is – we could really use your help this year. We're getting our butts kicked in almost every game. We need some of your offensive firepower."

"Yeah, I saw the game against the Bears."

"Really? You were there?"

"I kind of snuck in for a while," Logan said sheepishly. "Honestly, with the exception of that big center and the goalie, the Bears weren't that much better than you guys."

The look on Ryan's face was skeptical.

"But that goalie was awesome," Logan continued. "He had great hockey sense, as my dad would say. He wasn't just watching the puck, he was watching the plays develop, and you could tell he knew the position of every attacker on the ice."

"And, of course, we were short-handed for most of the game," Ryan pointed out.

"Yeah, Tyler has to learn to control himself," Logan agreed. "The aggressiveness is fine – he brings energy to the team. But hitting someone in the head just because they push you away is stupid. He needs to shrug that stuff off and walk away."

"Skate away," Ryan corrected.

"Yeah, skate away," repeated Logan, smiling for the first time.

Chapter 13

Logan's mom came home early from work to check on him and was surprised to find him in the street in front of the house skateboarding with a tall, blond-haired boy.

"Mom, this is Ryan. He brought over my math homework. Can Ryan and I go up the street to the skate park and practice our jumps on some of the ramps over there?"

"I'm feeling much better now," Logan added with a mischievous grin.

"I can see that," his mom said, noting the gleam in his eyes, in sharp contrast to the dullness that had been there earlier that morning.

"Just be home in an hour for dinner," she said as she watched him push off and glide down the street.

Joker bounded after him, anxious for some exercise too after a long day cooped up in the house.

Logan and Ryan turned right at the end of the block and then headed north through the industrial park. As they passed by Exotic Auto Repair, Logan pointed out the heavy-duty security fence topped by razor-sharp barbed wire that ran along one side of the building. As usual the business was dark, although the lights could have been on inside and were simply not visible because of the heavy blinds covering the windows. Clearly the owners of Exotic Auto didn't care about presenting an inviting image to their prospective customers.

Logan told Ryan about seeing a car being dropped off at 3:00 a.m. in the morning.

"I can't believe you were running around in the woods at that time of night," Ryan said.

"It wasn't my choice, believe me. But, seriously, why would a legitimate business be open in the middle of the night? And closed during the day and on weekends?"

Ryan just shook his head.

"And why," Logan continued, "would anyone need barbed wire? It looks like a prison fence."

"Well, maybe because the cars inside are really valuable. After all it does say *Exotic* Auto Repair, so maybe they specialize in pricey sports cars like Maseratis and Lamborghinis and stuff like that."

"Maybe," Logan said slowly, not sounding convinced.

"Do you remember what kind of car it was that you saw?" Ryan asked.

"No, I don't know a lot about cars. It was yellow though."

Ryan rolled his eyes in amusement, "Very helpful, Logan."

"Hey, it was dark," Logan laughed. "But I swear the driver looked like a gangbanger and I thought I saw the other guy hand him a wad of cash."

As they rolled down the street, Logan looked back over his shoulder at the dark, vacant yard of Exotic Auto and wondered, not for the first time, what was really going on inside that building.

Logan was in his bedroom doing homework when the doorbell rang. He heard the murmur of voices and then his mom call out his name. When he got to the front door, he was surprised to see Coach Brian standing there.

"Coach Sweeney wanted to talk to you, Logan," his mom said.

"Both of you actually," Coach Sweeney said.

"Can I get you something to drink, a soft drink perhaps?" Logan's mom asked as she started down the hallway towards the family room.

"No, I'm fine. Thank you."

A reading lamp had been pulled close to the sofa and a book was lying overturned on the ottoman. As Logan's mom bent to straighten the cushions, Coach Sweeney turned to Logan with an apologetic air. "I hope you won't be upset with Ryan for talking to me, Logan."

Logan could hear the thudding of his heart in his ears.

"But you have to understand one thing," the coach continued. "We're a hockey family. And I don't just mean that Ryan and I are family – even though he is my nephew – what I mean is that all the guys in this town who play hockey are like a family. We stick together. We play because we love the game, and the philosophy of the West Bend Hockey Club has always been that anyone who wants to play the game ought to be able to play it."

"In fact, we started a scholarship fund a couple of years ago for that very reason – to help deserving players who might not otherwise be able to afford the cost of the program. We know hockey is an expensive sport and not everyone has the same resources. Now the scholarship fund isn't that big right now – we've only put a little money aside. But we have a fundraiser scheduled for later in the season, and I thought maybe we could work out some kind of payment schedule . . ."

At this point in his speech, Coach Sweeney looked over at Logan's mom, a concerned expression on his face. "I hope I'm not overstepping my bounds here, Mrs. Michaud. It's just that Ryan said he got the distinct impression Logan was really missing hockey, and, honestly, I thought he didn't come to tryouts because he had gotten a better offer. I didn't realize he wasn't playing at all."

Logan's mom shook her head, "No. It's all right. I appreciate your interest and I'm sure Logan does too."

"In fact," she said with a slight smile, "interestingly enough, I was having a conversation on this very subject just yesterday."

Logan thought back to the uncomfortable moment at his grandparents' house.

"I thought if you knew about the scholarship fund and the possibility of a payment plan . . ." Coach Sweeney hesitated. "Well, I wanted to give you some options to think about, I guess."

Logan's mom stood for a moment her head bowed, lost in thought. The room grew silent and in the distance a car horn blared.

Finally she looked up, seemingly making up her mind about something. "I think I'd like to hear more about those options," she said.

Not even aware until that point that he'd been holding his breath, Logan slowly let the air out of his lungs.

Coach Sweeney seemed to relax too, "Maybe I will have that soft drink, if you don't mind."

As his mom went to grab a soda from the refrigerator, Logan retreated from the room, leaving the adults to talk about money issues. On his way out, he sent up a silent prayer to his dad. *Dad, if you can help in any way, I'd be really grateful. And, I promise, if I get a chance to play hockey this year, I'll work extra hard to make you proud.*

Chapter 14

Thirty minutes later, Logan's mom knocked on his door and came in and sat down on the bed.

"Coach Sweeney is a nice man," she said.

"Yeah, I think all the players on the team really like him."

"Honey, I want you to know I'll do everything I can to make this happen. I know how difficult this past year has been and I know how much you love hockey and . . . ."

His mom took a deep breath, "Coach Sweeney says that with uniform and miscellaneous fees the total cost to play for one year is around $3,400."

Logan felt a jolt of electricity go through him. Even though he expected the fees to be high, it was still a shock to hear the actual number.

"I can probably swing $1,000," his mom said. "And I'm hoping to borrow another $1,000 from your grandparents. Coach Sweeney said he would talk to the scholarship committee to see how much they'd be willing to contribute."

"And I have my job at Perelli's," Logan added. "I can chip in something from that."

"Well, with practices and games I'm not sure how much time you'll have for a part-time job. But, we'll see. Maybe in the summer. Coach Sweeney suggested that we might be able to work out a payment plan for the balance."

A shiver of excitement danced up Logan's spine. *This could actually work, he thought.*

"There's just one thing," his mom said.

Logan tensed, waiting for the hammer to fall.

"This arrangement will only cover us for one year," his mom said. "Next year we'll have to come up with another $3,400 and then another $3,400 the year after that."

She sighed, "There won't be much money left over to put away into savings. We do have the proceeds from your dad's insurance policy but those funds are earmarked for your college education and I won't touch them under any circumstances."

Logan wasn't sure what to say so he sat quietly waiting for her to continue.

His mom looked down at her hands. "It probably means that we'll have to keep renting this house for a while. I was hoping to save enough money for a down payment on a house of our own but now I think it will take a little longer than I expected."

When she looked back up, there was a question in her eyes.

"I don't mind living here, Mom," Logan exclaimed. "Really, I don't. I mean, why would I? The house is nice and it's close to the rink. Plus it's close to Perelli's and the school too. When you think about it, it's kind of perfect. Really, it's a great house."

His mom laughed, "Well, I'm not sure I'd call it a *great* house. It's old and small and located right next to an industrial park. But I guess it will have to do . . . for a while anyway."

Logan was stacking heads of lettuce, arranging them in neat precise rows, when Mr. Perelli walked over to stand next to him. Mr. Perelli was a short, stocky man who always wore a dark green shirt with the name "Perelli's Market" embroidered on the pocket. He looked more like a former wrestler than the hockey player he'd actually been back during his high school days at West Bend High.

He'd been good too, Logan had heard. Logan imagined getting checked into the boards by a young Mr. Perelli would not have been a pleasant experience.

"How do you like working here, Logan?" Mr. Perelli asked.

"I like it just fine, Mr. Perelli," Logan answered.

"It's not interfering with your school work now is it?"

"No, I'm keeping up alright."

Mr. Perelli nodded his head up and down looking a bit like a bobble head doll.

Logan waited for him to move off and when Mr. Perelli just continued to stand there wondered what was on his mind.

I hope I haven't screwed up somehow, Logan thought, momentarily panicked.

"You know, I hear there's a chance you might be playing for the Warriors' Pee Wee team."

Logan glanced up, surprised.

This is a small town, he thought.

"I talked to Coach Sweeney this morning and he told me he's trying to recruit you for the team." Mr. Pereilli paused, "Listen, I have a proposition for you. What if I advance you some money towards your hockey fees, say $500 or so, and then gave you some time to work it off?"

Logan was speechless.

"What do I pay you now anyway? Ten bucks an hour? At that rate, if you came in maybe two hours a week, it would take about six months to pay off your debt. We could work around your hockey schedule, and if things started to become too much, we could postpone repayment until the season was over or even summer. What do you think?"

"I think that's very generous. Are you sure?"

"Absolutely sure," Mr. Perelli smiled broadly and clapped Logan on the back. "There's just one condition though."

"What's that?"

"I want you to give me a copy of your hockey schedule because, if I have time and it's okay with you, I'd like to come watch a game or two."

He started to walk away and then turned back and winked, "You see I've heard, as far as hockey skills go, the apple didn't fall far from the tree."

After his shift at Perelli's Market was over, Logan raced home to tell his mom the news. He found her in the kitchen fixing dinner. Pieces of chicken were sizzling in a stir-fry pan and freshly chopped vegetables ready to be tossed in were piled high on the cutting board nearby.

She listened patiently and then told him her good news. According to Coach Sweeney, the scholarship committee had voted to award Logan a small scholarship to help defray the cost of his hockey fees.

"Really?"

"Now it's not much, but the Hockey Club has also agreed to a very reasonable payment plan, and . . . since your grandparents want to give you a combined early Christmas and birthday present . . . ."

She looked over at his eager face and broke into a smile. Logan gave a whoop that sent Joker running in circles, his tail wagging in excitement.

"Thanks, mom," he said as he gave her a big hug.

"Oh, and Coach Sweeney dropped something off for you. I put it in your room."

Logan sprinted back to his bedroom and stopped dead in his tracks in the doorway. Lying there on his bed was a cobalt blue and black Warriors jersey with the number 9 stenciled on the back.

"By the way," his mom yelled from the kitchen, "there's a practice tomorrow and a game on Saturday so maybe after dinner you should get started on your homework."

"Okay, Mom," he yelled back. "Let's eat right now 'cause I have a ton of math homework tonight!"

Chapter 15

The next few days were a blur of activity. Logan had a chapter test in math and a quiz on photosynthesis in science. He also had to write an English paper on a short story his class had read.

On Tuesday Coach Sweeney ran a fast-paced practice. He slotted Logan on the first line at right wing with Ryan in the center position. To Logan's surprise and relief, none of his new teammates seemed to question his sudden presence on the team. It was as if, by some unspoken agreement, they were willing to overlook the fact that he had bypassed tryouts because they knew how much the team needed him. No one, not even Tyler, disputed his talent. Besides, the team still hadn't notched its first win of the season and most of the players were getting tired of losing.

The game on Saturday was against the Ice Dogs, a solid middle-of-the-pack team that was good but not unbeatable. Feeling anxious, Logan arrived at the rink early, and by the time the first of his teammates had wandered into the locker room, he was almost fully dressed.

The rest of the team slowly trickled in and finally Coach Brian and Coach Matt, clipboards in hand, popped in to give a brief pep talk. When the team skated out onto the ice to scattered applause from the stands, Logan was grateful just to get his feet moving. The anticipation of this moment had built inside him to a fever pitch. He whipped around the Warriors' half of the ice at breakneck speed for a couple of laps and then dropped in front of the bench for stretches. Glancing up into the stands once, he thought he saw the blond, pony-haired profile of Megan. He knew his grandparents would be coming to the game too.

Logan felt the weight of the expectations of so many others on his shoulders: his mom who was sacrificing so much so that he could play; his coach who had lobbied to get him a scholarship; his teammates who were looking to him to score and even Mr. Perelli who had taken an interest in him and advanced him money for his hockey fees. Logan didn't want to disappoint any of them. And then there was the thought of his father up there looking down on him. His prayers about playing hockey had been answered, and in his heart, he believed his father had had something to do with that.

Logan was so focused on his thoughts that as he skated out to the centerline for the opening face-off the raucous sounds of the rink receded into the distance. Time slowed and the lights in the rink seemed to dim. His body, perfectly still, was hunched over his stick. His eyes were glued to the black rubber disk clasped in the referee's hand. Then the referee released the puck and it seemed to float down gently until, *smack*, the sights and sounds of the rink exploded back to life.

Both centers slashed furiously trying to wrest control of the puck from each other until it skittered sideways to Dylan, the Warriors' left winger. Dylan picked it up and shot the puck forward along the boards where an Ice Dog defenseman chased it down. He in turn wrapped it back around the net to his teammate who caught it just as Logan charged into the corner.

Slapping at the puck, Logan managed to jostle it loose, and once he had control he fired it to Ryan who was positioned perfectly right in front of the net.

Unfortunately, the hard shot caused the puck to dance off Ryan's stick and an Ice Dog picked it up and headed back up the ice towards the Warriors' goal. Logan sprinted after him and caught up with him a few feet outside the Warriors' blue line. Leaning into his opponent's body he knocked him off balance and poked the puck off to the side. James Toth, one of the Warriors' defensemen, picked it up and dropped back.

Meanwhile Logan had spun around and reversed direction and was now racing back towards the Ice Dogs' goal. James fired a pass that reached Logan just as he crossed the red line. Logan charged toward one defenseman and then swung wide to his left at the last possible moment. With a burst of speed, he skated past his opponent and now the only thing between Logan and the goal was a solitary Ice Dog. The other skater moved to block but before he was able to get into position, Logan snapped his wrist and fired. The move caught the Ice Dog goalie off guard – he wasn't expecting a shot from quite so far out. The goalie dropped to his knees, but it was too late. The puck had slipped between his legs. *Goal!*

Logan raised a triumphant arm in the air as a roar went up from the crowd. Ryan and the rest of his linemates crowded around him for a celebratory group hug, then the whole group skated past the bench for the obligatory glove taps. Coach Brian motioned for them to stay out on the ice, so once again the lines and the referee took their positions at center ice.

Logan's heart was beating fast in his chest and adrenaline was racing through his body as he bent over his stick once again. But this time the worry and anxiety had been pushed to the side. This time the sounds of the rink filled his head. He allowed himself a small smile as he listened to the cheers from the stands and words of encouragement from his teammates on the bench. Then referee raised his arm and Logan tensed his body ready to quickly jump forward, eager to feel the weight of the puck on his stick again.

Chapter 16

The mood in the locker room after the game was jubilant. The Warriors had finally posted their first win of the season, thanks in no small part to Logan who had scored a hat trick and accounted for 3 of the team's 4 goals. As was their custom, the team remained in their uniforms until after Coach Brian and Coach Matt gave their post-game analysis and wrap-up. Coach Brian kept it brief, highlighting the defensive play of the goalie and, of course, Logan's outstanding effort on offense.

Then the coaches left and the locker room erupted into excited chatter. There was plenty of good-natured shoving and horseplay as James and Dylan played a game of keep away with one of Tyler's game socks and Carlos demonstrated his stick handling skills on a clump of balled up hockey tape.

Logan sat quietly on the bench unlacing his skates, a big smile plastered on his face. This is what he loved so much about hockey – this feeling of brotherhood and camaraderie, this feeling of doing battle with his fellow warriors and emerging from the fray exhausted but victorious. In his heart Logan knew that no matter how much his skills might have tipped the balance in favor of a win, he couldn't do it alone. He needed his teammates as much as they needed him. In all the times that he and his parents had moved in Canada – and they had moved frequently in his short life – he had always felt a sense of belonging once he found his team. And now he'd found his team. For the first time since moving to West Bend, he finally felt as if he truly belonged somewhere.

"Hey, you wanna hang out after the game?" Ryan asked as he flopped down on the bench next to Logan.

"Sure."

"I can't believe that breakaway you scored on. That was a thing of beauty," Ryan said, referring to the play in the third period when Logan had streaked the length of the ice virtually unopposed and then flipped the puck over the goalie's shoulder at the last second.

Logan laughed, "I think Dylan might've accidently tripped one of their defensemen, but the ref didn't see it."

"Well, it's about time one of those referee calls went our way."

"Believe me," Logan said smiling. "I'm not complaining."

Ryan went home to shower and then his dad dropped him off at Logan's house around 4:00 p.m. The two boys decided to explore the neighborhood on their skateboards, so they locked Joker in the house and cut across the woods in Logan's backyard, intent on checking out the strange goings-on at Exotic Auto.

The sun was bright and the air was crisp with only a few wispy clouds scudding across the expanse of clear blue sky. As Logan and Ryan skated past the front of the building, they noticed a truck and an old junker parked outside. Circling around the block, they came up through an alley and approached from the rear. There was a back door that opened onto the alley and two small windows on either side that appeared to have been covered over with black paint. A dumpster was pushed up against the wall to the right of the door.

"You know, you can tell a lot about people by what they throw away in their garbage," Logan said.

"Okay, Detective Michaud, why don't you go and have a look."

Logan crept over to the metal bin and slowly lifted up the cover. Inside was a foul mix of half-eaten food, fast food wrappers, empty drink cups and plastic bags tied with yellow tape.

"Any dead bodies in there?" whispered Ryan who had sidled up beside him.

Logan jumped. "Real funny."

As they moved closer to the door, they could hear the sounds of machinery inside. The faint odor of paint wafted through a large vent directly above the door.

Suddenly they heard the sound of a voice on the other side of the door and raced to hide behind a wooden fence running the length of the alley. Peering through cracks in the slats, they saw a large, burly man with a black apron covered in paint splatters step out and heard him yell back to someone inside, "I'm just going out for a smoke." A white facemask was hanging from the guy's neck and his muscular arms and lower legs were covered in tattoos. He looked exactly like someone you wouldn't want to run into in an alley, especially not a dark one.

He was keeping the door open with his hip while he took drags off his cigarette, and from their angle Logan and Ryan could see past him into the interior of the building. At the end of a long hallway was a center room with white walls and bright lights. There was nothing in there except two long tables with large metal pieces on top. The place had the white sterile look of an operating room.

Next to the tables were spray guns with hoses attached. It looked as if the workers had just finished spraying the doors of a car and had left them out to dry.

"Hey, !@#$&, close the door. You're letting dirt in," a voice inside yelled, punctuating his command with an expletive.

"!@#$&," responded the guy in the alley in kind, and then he flicked the cigarette to the ground and crushed it under the heel of his boot. The door swung shut and locked with a click.

Ryan and Logan held their breath for a couple of seconds before Ryan whispered, "Looks like they're painting cars in there."

"Yeah."

"I'm pretty sure that's not illegal."

"I know but . . . " Logan's voice trailed off. "These guys don't look like legitimate mechanics or whatever."

"What is a legitimate mechanic supposed to look like?" Ryan asked.

"I don't know but not like he should be sitting in a cell in Leavenworth or something."

"I think you're letting your imagination run wild," Ryan said. "Maybe he's an ex-con who did his time and now he has a real job."

"Maybe. It's just that I know what I saw the other night and it was really weird. Who drops off a car at 3:00 a.m. in the morning anyway? And I swear, it looked like the guy handed the driver a wad of cash?"

"Could you *swear* it was cash?" Ryan asked.

"Well, no," Logan admitted. "It was too dark and I was too far away. But I doubt it was a bag of chocolate chip cookies!"

Ryan snorted in amusement.

"Do you want to say something to Coach Brian?" Ryan asked. "He could keep an eye on the place, drive by occasionally – even though he doesn't work the late shift."

"No, probably not," Logan said. "Like you said, it's probably just my vivid imagination. There could be a reasonable explanation for most of this stuff."

Ryan nodded his head. "Yeah, like, if they repair expensive cars, maybe they need the security of a chain link fence. You know, to protect their property."

"And because they specialize in high-end cars," Logan added, "maybe that explains why they don't have regular hours. They might see people by appointment only or something."

The two boys emerged from behind the fence and started back down the alley heading away from the shop. Logan looked over at Ryan who was gliding alongside him and asked, "You want to go back to my house and play some video games? I have the latest version of Vigilante Town."

"We could track down some fake bad guys and put them away – since it doesn't seem to be happening in real life," he added with a grin.

Ryan laughed. "Trust me, Logan. I've lived in this town my whole life. West Bend isn't exciting enough to attract big-time criminals. Video games are the only way you'll run across any action around here."

Chapter 17

The following week the Warriors recorded two more victories, including a hard-fought win against the second place Huskies. Logan had 2 goals and 2 assists in that game and even played defense in the final period as the Warriors struggled to preserve their two-goal lead.

Logan ran into Megan in the hallway on Thursday and asked how her soccer season was going.

"Well, we've won three games already so we're definitely ahead of last season. But we still have an open spot on the team for Joker, if he's interested," she added, smiling. "We could really use someone with his kind of speed."

On Friday after school, Logan unloaded boxes and stacked fruits and vegetables at Perelli's until 6:00 p.m. when his shift ended. He had a big weekend of hockey coming up, a practice on Saturday and then a rematch against the unbeaten Bears on Sunday. Walking home in the gathering dusk, he was about two blocks from his house when he abruptly stopped in the middle of the sidewalk. Parked up the street in the alley alongside Exotic Auto was a large box truck. Curious, Logan decided to take a detour and instead of turning left, he turned right and retraced the steps he and Ryan had taken the previous Saturday and approached the truck from the opposite end of the alley. He stayed in the shadows to keep out of sight, and once he reached the fence, he crept behind it and moved closer until he was about 15 feet away.

The truck's motor was running but there was no one around. Then the door to the alley opened and two men stepped out. One guy Logan recognized as the man who'd been smoking in the alley that day, but the other guy he'd never seen before.

The smoker guy picked up a piece of cardboard from the ground and jammed it into the frame of the door near the handle. The paper prevented the door from closing all the way and locking. The other guy got behind the wheel of the truck and suddenly there was a whining sound and the back door of the truck slowly began to descend until the top of the door was touching the ground, forming a kind of ramp.

Logan could now see the shape of what looked like a car in the interior of the truck. The car appeared to be covered with a plastic tarp. The driver got out and walked around to the back of the truck and manually unlocked and removed two clamps that were holding the rear tires in place. Then he ripped off the tarp to reveal a small white sports car, a sleek two-seater, with the symbol of a silver horse rearing up on its hind legs on its back end.

The smoker guy whistled, "Wow, that's a beaut. How much does one of these babies go for?"

The driver laughed, "What's that saying? If you have to ask, you probably can't afford it."

Smoker guy just stared at him, not cracking a smile, "The white color looks sharp. What color are we painting it?"

"Whatever the buyer wants, which in this case is black."

"When do you need it?"

"Wednesday. You got five days to work your magic."

"Is that when you're making your next delivery?"

"Nah, we got a shipment coming in tomorrow night. A real sweet Porsche."

"Nothing tonight?"

"Nope, you got the night off tonight, Frankie. Go have some fun."

The car was shifted over to the right side in the extra wide truck body and Frankie climbed up in the back.

"Be careful," the driver warned. "Don't scratch the door or that'll cost you ten grand, easy." He snickered and watched as Frankie carefully maneuvered the sports car down the ramp and into the alley.

Once the car was safely out, the driver climbed back into the cab of the truck, and with the press of a button, hydraulic arms started lifting the ramp up off the ground and back into position, closing up the back of the truck like a giant clam snapping shut.

Then with a slight lurch, the truck moved down the alley and turned left at the street. The sports car followed behind it, but it turned right and then right again into the driveway of Exotic Auto. Just as the sports car was turning, Logan noticed the license plate in the back. But by the time his brain registered the idea that he should copy the numbers down, the car had completed its turn and the plate was out of view.

I can't believe how stupid I am! Logan thought, chastising himself. I could have given Coach Brian the license plate and he could have run the numbers or something,

Logan stayed behind the fence for another ten minutes, waiting to see if anyone returned to check on the alley door, but to his surprise Frankie seemed to have forgotten that he'd wedged the door open and left it unlocked. Finally Logan emerged from his hiding spot and backtracked down the alley, heading home before it got too dark and his mom started to worry.

Chapter 18

Later that night Logan sat at the computer in the family room and typed the words "sports cars" into the computer's search engine. He scrolled through images of different makes and models until he finally spied the silver horse logo.

"Ferrari," he muttered under his breath. Then he clicked on the manufacturer's website and searched until he found a car that looked identical to the one he'd seen in the alley. When he saw the price tag, he gasped. The car cost almost $200,000 brand new!

That's crazy, Logan said to himself. Why would someone paint over an expensive car like that, especially one that was in pristine condition? If someone wanted a black car, they could simply buy a black car.

Then Logan remembered the comment the driver had made to Frankie, about how if someone had to ask the price of something, they probably couldn't afford it.

Yeah, Logan thought. That's true. People who can afford to buy a car like that, buy the color they want. They don't repaint. And why was the car being shipped in an old truck like that? There was obviously nothing wrong with the engine because Frankie was able to drive it from the alley to the front of the building. Why didn't they just drive the car to the shop in the first place to get it repainted?

Suddenly Logan snapped his fingers. *Wait a minute, he thought. That truck had some kind of name on the side of it.*

The image of the truck turning onto the street flashed in his brain. In his mind's eye he saw the words "Bittman Furniture" printed in bold black letters on the side panel.

Weirder and weirder, Logan thought. An expensive car like that in a furniture truck? It doesn't make sense. None of it makes sense. I sure wish I'd gotten that license plate number, he thought again, for the zillionth time.

By the time Logan finished his research on the Internet, it was late. He paused at the door to his mom's bedroom where she was sitting up in bed, propped up by pillows and reading a book.

"'Night, Mom."

"Goodnight, honey. Did you turn out the lights in the family room?"

"Yep, I did, and I turned off the computer too."

Joker padded softly behind Logan as he made his way to his bedroom. The faithful dog lay down on the carpet next to Logan's bed like a sentry guarding his post. Logan turned out the lights and climbed into bed, but despite the lateness of the hour, sleep eluded him. His mind was churning with thoughts of sports cars and tattooed men who looked like they belonged behind prison bars but were instead working just two streets away.

Am I really just imagining things like Ryan said? he wondered. Maybe I've played too many video games and now I'm seeing bad guys around every corner.

His last thought before he drifted off to sleep was of a certain license plate number on a certain sports car and how much he regretted not copying that number down.

Logan awoke with a start and for a moment stared in confusion at the ceiling of his room.

What time is it? His sleepy brain struggled to focus.

The clock face read 4:58 a.m. Logan stole over to the window and parted the curtains. Off in the distance soft tendrils of light heralded the coming of the morning sun. As he looked at the sky, which seemed a little less ominous in the weak morning light, he thought about the unlocked door in the alley behind Exotic Auto.

It would take ten minutes to check and see if it is still unlocked, he thought. And another ten minutes to sneak in and get the license plate number off the car.

He remembered the truck driver telling Frankie that they weren't expecting any shipments and to take the night off, so he wasn't worried anyone would be around to see him. Plus, he'd take a small flashlight so he didn't have to turn any lights on.

Logan glanced over at Joker who had briefly awoken when he got out of bed and was now fast asleep again. He'd have to leave Joker in the house, even though he really wouldn't mind a four-legged bodyguard.

But what if Joker spotted a cat or something and started barking? Logan thought. No, he'll have to stay behind.

Logan slipped out of the room without waking Joker again and debated whether to leave by the front or the back door. He decided to take the shortcut through the backyard, and as he passed through the kitchen, he grabbed a small flashlight from one of the drawers and his sweatshirt, which was hanging on the back of a chair.

The early morning air was chilly and he shivered as he slowly closed the door. Besides his sweatshirt, he was wearing grey sweatpants, a T-shirt and his black and grey skateboarding low tops. He waited a bit to let his eyes adjust to the gloom, even though in the last 15 minutes or so the sky had brightened at least a shade. He quickly made his way through the woods in back and stopped at the tree line on the other side.

Glancing both ways and seeing no one on the street, he raced across to the entrance to the alley. There was a dim light above the alley door, and as he got closer, he could see the cardboard paper still sticking out.

Clearly, this Frankie is not the sharpest knife in the drawer, Logan thought.

Logan put his ear to the door and listened for sounds. Hearing none, he slowly and quietly pulled the door open and slipped through, careful to replace the cardboard in the crack to keep the door from clicking shut. The interior of the building was pitch black, so Logan clicked on his small flashlight to navigate his way down the corridor.

The paint fumes became stronger as he moved towards the interior rooms. The back corridor led into the sterile white room he and Ryan had observed from the alley with its dangling spray guns and big metal tables. The room was empty now with the exception of the spray guns, which were still tethered to the ceiling. He weaved around them and turned left into an open door that led to the main garage. As he entered the garage, his flashlight played over the big open space. It too was empty with one important exception – parked off to the side was the very sleek, very shiny and very expensive white Ferrari sports car.

Chapter 19

Logan tiptoed to the rear of the car and shined his flashlight on the license plate. It read: JGM 15.

At least it's an easy one to remember, Logan thought, since I forgot to bring something to write it down on. Clearly, I'm not too good at this detective thing either.

As he stood there looking at the license plate and trying to commit it to memory, he became aware of a rhythmic buzzing sound. He clicked off the light and listened.

What is that? he wondered.

As he strained to hear, it suddenly dawned on him that what he was hearing was the sound of someone snoring.

Oh, no! Logan thought. There's someone else in here. Or maybe something else in here – like a guard dog!

Logan could feel the panic rising up in his chest. He moved to the other side of the car, as far away from the snoring sounds as he could possibly get, and as he brushed past a low cabinet, his sleeve caught on something and he heard the sound of metal clanging to the floor.

Immediately the snoring sounds stopped and he knew he'd awoken whoever *or whatever* had been sleeping. An interior light flashed on in one of the back offices and shed just enough light to reveal a door off to Logan's right. It was the closest place he could see to hide since he knew he couldn't make it the length of the garage to the back corridor. Logan quickly darted through the door and found himself in an extra large storage closet filled with paint cans, buckets and other painting supplies. Over in the corner was a large pile of used drop cloths and Logan dove behind it just as the interior of the garage was flooded with an intensely bright light.

119

He could hear footsteps moving around the perimeter of the garage, stopping and starting occasionally as if someone were checking around corners and behind columns. He burrowed deeper into the pile and pulled the top cloth over himself so that he was completely covered. The footsteps stopped just outside the storage closet door and Logan squeezed his eyes shut, hoping that would help make him invisible. Then the footsteps moved on and he heard the sound of a metal object being picked up off the floor.

"Now, how the !@#$& did you get there?" he heard a voice say.

The unknown person continued his search and then moved off in the direction of the back door.

Uh oh, Logan thought. Once he discovers the back door wedged open, he'll get even more suspicious.

Sure enough, after a few minutes Logan heard the back door being opened and then slammed shut with a click. When the person returned to the center garage, Logan could hear the distinctive beeping sounds of numbers being punched into a cell phone.

"Hey Frankie, you need to get down here, man. I think we had a break-in."

Logan was too far away to hear Frankie's response, but when he peeked out from under his covers, he saw a tall skinny guy with long hair and sagging jeans, talking on his cell phone with his back to him.

Logan's eyes widened in shock when he saw what the guy was holding in his other hand. A black handgun.

"No, I don't know if anything was taken, but the back door was open."

The guy listened and then said, "Well, not like completely open but someone had put some paper in there so it wouldn't shut all the way."

After he listened some more, the skinny guy yelled angrily into the phone, "Are you !@#$& kidding me? Why'd you do that, you moron? Don't you know anyone could've walked in here while I was sleeping?"

There was another pause and then he said, "No, I didn't see anyone but I heard something, although now I'm thinking it was probably just a big rat. Listen why don't you haul your lazy !@#$& out of bed and come down here so we can get started on this car. Oh, and bring some food with you 'cause I'm starving."

With that parting shot the guy clicked off his phone and walked over to an office just off the garage space. Now that the lights were on, Logan could see that one entire wall of the office was clear glass, allowing its occupants to oversee the work going on in the garage. He saw the skinny guy grab a can of something from a small refrigerator and use a remote to snap on a television set. Then the guy settled into a chair that was angled so he was half facing the well-lit center space.

With a sinking heart, Logan realized he was trapped. With the lights on, the guy would immediately see if Logan left his hiding spot and tried to make a run for the back door.

Yet the man had said they needed to start painting the car, Logan thought. Surely they'll need these drop cloths I'm hiding under.

Logan lowered his head, unsure of what to do. He didn't know how soon the other guy would show up or even the number of guys that worked in the garage. He wondered if they all carried guns. He figured his only chance was to stay put and hope skinny guy left to use the bathroom or something at which point he'd try to make a break for it.

Chapter 20

Logan's mother, Anne Michaud, was seated on the family room sofa, staring blindly at the carpet, her hands twisting a crumpled tissue. The small house was abuzz with activity: police officers milling about, their walkie-talkies crackling with sound; Grandpa Frank standing by the window deep in conversation with one of the officers who was writing something in a small notebook; and Nona in the kitchen making another pot of coffee.

Coach Brian Sweeney eased down into a chair next to Anne, the black Warriors jacket he normally wore during the games now replaced by the crisp blue uniform of a police lieutenant. His face bore an expression of concern.

When she had first awoken and realized Logan was missing, Anne Michaud had called her parents, and after an anxious hour of searching the neighborhood, they had called the police.

"So you're sure the back door would have been locked?" he asked gently.

"Yes, it's always locked at night," she said.

"I remember he stopped by my room to say goodnight before he went to bed," she added, her eyes starting to well up with tears. "I asked if he'd turned off the lights and he said he had and that he'd shut off the computer too."

"So he was on the computer before he went to bed last night?"

"Yes."

"Do you know what he was doing on the computer? What he was looking at?"

"No, not really."

"Does he ever chat online with anyone? You know, other kids and such?"

Anne Michaud's hand flew up and covered her mouth as the implication of his question suddenly dawned on her.

"You don't think he was talking online to some . . . some . . . bad . . ." She couldn't bring herself to finish the sentence.

Lt. Sweeney shook his head. "Knowing Logan, that doesn't seem likely, but it's something we should definitely check out. Would it be all right with you if one of our experts took a look at your computer?"

"Of course. Do whatever you need to do."

As Lt. Sweeney rose to give instructions to one of his officers, Grandpa Frank moved over to stand next to Anne. He bent down and said quietly, "The police have finished canvassing the neighbors and no one remembers seeing anything. Most of them were just getting up when the police knocked on their doors."

"I don't understand how this could have happened," she said, her voice trembling.

"The police seem to think Logan left willingly, otherwise they think Joker would have sounded some kind of alarm," Grandpa Frank said.

"Yes, he usually sleeps right by Logan's bed at night. In fact, Joker's the one who came and woke me up. He was whining and wanting to go out. I think he sensed something was wrong."

"What happened when you let him out?"

"I don't really remember. He ran into the woods in back and was gone awhile, but then he came back."

A female police officer followed Lt. Sweeney into the room and immediately went over to the computer desk in the corner and sat down. After inquiring about the computer's passwords, she quickly began tapping keys on the keyboard.

Lt. Sweeney rejoined Anne Michaud and Grandpa Frank over by the sofa.

"Can you give me a list of Logan's friends? Anyone he would have talked to recently? We'll probably want to check with them," he said.

"He really only knows the boys on the hockey team. There's one boy, Ryan, who's been over here a few times," she added.

Lt. Sweeney left again to make a phone call and when he returned he said, "I just spoke with Ryan. He doesn't remember Logan mentioning anything about talking to people on the Internet or going into any chat rooms. He said when he was over here they mostly played video games or skateboarded around neighborhood."

Grandpa Frank cleared his throat. "Do you think it's possible Logan simply ran away?" he asked hesitantly. "I mean, I know this past year has been rough with Jon's death and the move and all. Maybe he was overwhelmed and unhappy and . . . ." His voice trailed off, leaving the unspoken words hanging in the air.

"No," Anne Michaud said firmly. "I don't believe it. Logan was excited about playing hockey again and he was happy to be on the team. He was doing well in school, making friends. I just don't believe he would run away. It's only the two of us and he wouldn't simply leave . . . I know he wouldn't."

"I think it's highly unlikely too," Lt. Sweeney agreed. "Usually kids who run away take something with them, whether it's extra clothes, food, money – even a toothbrush. It doesn't appear that anything's missing from the house, except maybe a sweatshirt from the kitchen. That tells me wherever Logan was going, he was intending to come back."

"Lieutenant," the computer expert interrupted, swiveling in her chair to face the group.

"Got anything?" Lt. Sweeney asked.

"It looks pretty clean, sir," she said. "I checked the history for the last 12 months and there's no evidence of any chat room conversations or any other kind of suspicious Internet activity for that matter. It's mostly visits to hockey websites and maybe some searches for school-related stuff. You know, like research for a school paper or something."

"Can you tell what he was looking at last night?" Lt. Sweeney asked.

"Sure, it looks like he was looking at pictures of sports cars. And he visited the Ferrari website and looked at some of their models. Seems like typical boy stuff to me."

Lt. Sweeney turned to Anne Michaud, "Is Logan interested in sports cars?"

"Not to my knowledge. But he plays those video games. Don't they have sports cars in them?"

"Yeah," Lt. Sweeney sighed. "He was probably checking out some car he saw in a video game. Like the officer said, typical boy stuff."

Chapter 21

Logan shifted under the mound of drop cloths, trying to relieve the pressure on his left leg where a cramp was forming. He'd been hiding in the storage closet for what seemed like hours now and the skinny guy watching television hadn't moved a muscle. At least Logan *thought* he was watching television.

For all I know, he's sound asleep in there, Logan said to himself, frustrated.

Whereas the back of the shop was dark and windowless, the front space had skylights set high in the garage's ceiling, and the morning light was starting to stream through in earnest.

Logan had done his best to bury himself in the nest of stiff, paint-splattered cloths and he was pretty sure no one would be able to see him, even someone standing on the door's threshold, as long as the lights remained off. But if anyone came in and turned on the light – well, then he was probably doomed.

Finally he heard the sound of rattling metal.

Uh oh, thought Logan. Sounds like someone's opening the driveway fence.

He heard the motor of a vehicle being shut off and then the slamming of a door.

Seconds later a key was inserted into a side door and he heard the squeak of hinges as the door opened. Logan peeked out and saw skinny guy jump up from his chair and hurry out into the central garage area. He could see Frankie with a couple of fast food bags in his hand walking over to meet him.

"Can't you go somewhere other than Zippy's Burgers for once?" skinny guy said angrily. "I've had burgers for like five days in a row."

"Who cares?" Frankie sneered. "Do you see anyone who gives a !@#$&?"

"Besides, I like their fries," he added. "If you want something else take the truck and go get it."

With that, he tossed a set of keys to the other guy who grabbed them in midair and stuffed them in his pocket.

"Nah," skinny guy said, snatching one of the bags from Frankie and turning on his heel. "I'll suffer through another burger."

Both men went into the glass-walled office and Logan could see them spread their lunches out on a desk and start eating. The sound of the television in the background muted their conversation. They stayed in the office for at least half an hour, and when they were finished, they gathered up their crumpled wrappers and tossed them at a wastebasket on the other side of the room like a couple of point guards trying to sink a three-pointer.

Then skinny guy disappeared into another room in the back while Frankie stayed behind, his feet propped up on a table, glued to something on the television screen.

Suddenly Logan tensed. He could see skinny guy returning from the back and he was heading straight for the storage closet where Logan was hiding.

"C'mon, let's get started," he yelled over his shoulder.

Just before reaching the closet, he veered off to the right and Logan heard the sound of a cabinet door being opened and then water running. It sounded like the guy was filling a bucket with water.

"Take the license plate off," skinny guy ordered. He seemed to be the one in charge.

Logan couldn't see what was happening but based on the sounds coming through the door, he guessed they were washing the Ferrari. Suddenly skinny guy said, "Go get some dry rags from the closet," and Logan heard Frankie enter the storage room and take two steps towards one of the shelving units. Logan squeezed his eyes shut and held his breath. The guy was so close Logan could smell the stale scent of smoke on his clothes. Logan was convinced he was about to be discovered, but fortunately Frankie didn't bother to snap on the lights and simply grabbed a couple of rags and left.

Logan slowly exhaled. His heart was beating so loudly in his chest he couldn't believe the guys outside couldn't hear it. Then someone turned on a radio and the twang of a country music song drowned out everything else.

Logan guessed the two guys spent about an hour washing and drying the sports car, although it was difficult to tell because time seemed to crawl at a snail's pace. At one point Logan poked his head up and noticed a clock on the far wall of the garage. The time was 12:17 p.m.

"Seven hours?" Logan thought incredulously. "Have I really been here for seven hours?"

Then he remembered he had hockey practice at 3:00 p.m. The thought of practice led to thoughts of home and suddenly a sickening realization hit him. His mom must be wondering where he was.

What did she think when she woke up and found me gone? he asked himself. Did she think I was kidnapped or ran away? She must be frantic with worry not knowing where I am. I wonder if she called the police.

Logan was so busy with his thoughts he didn't realize that Frankie was standing in front of the storage room door until he heard the sound of his voice.

"What grade do you want?" he asked. "1000? 2000?" Frankie's hand was resting casually on the light switch ready to turn it on.

"It's not in there, you moron. The sandpaper's in the last drawer on the end."

As Frankie moved off, another country song came on and the garage was once again filled with the country drawl of someone singing about guns, dogs and pickup trucks.

The two men continued to work, taking breaks occasionally but never at the same time. Logan watched as the hands on the clock slowly crept around the clock face. When he heard a low rumbling in his stomach, he was reminded that he hadn't eaten anything all day.

Are these guys ever going to quit working? he wondered. Hopefully they'll get hungry again and stop for dinner. I wonder if one of them sleeps here every night.

Logan didn't relish the thought of having to wait until someone fell asleep before he could attempt an escape, but even that scenario was vastly preferable to the alternative – having one of them walk in the closet, flick on the light and discover his hiding spot. And that, he figured, could happen at any time.

Chapter 22

By midafternoon, a missing person's report had been filed and all on-duty police officers in the immediate vicinity had been notified of Logan's disappearance. In addition, a recent photograph of Logan had been distributed to the patrol cars in the area for use during their rounds.

At first, Lt. Sweeney had harbored the small hope that Logan had simply run off, perhaps to punish his mother for some imagined wrong, but as the day wore on and with no sign of Logan, he was beginning to fear something more ominous had happened. Although he'd been coaching Logan for a couple of weeks now and had spoken with him a few times, Lt. Sweeney had to admit he really didn't know the boy all that well. Both mother and son had lived in West Bend only a few months and he knew the family had money issues. Perhaps there were other family secrets that were just now starting to surface.

Yet the more time he spent with Anne Michaud, the more he began to doubt she was holding anything back. Brian Sweeney had been a police officer for almost fifteen years and during that time he'd gotten pretty good at reading people. And his read on Anne Michaud was that she was truly perplexed by Logan's disappearance and had no idea where he was or why he had taken off. The fear and anguish he saw on her face was not something easily faked.

Plus, there was the fact that Logan was Frank and Marjorie Schneider's grandson. The Schneiders had lived in West Bend for years and Brian Sweeney knew them well. Surely if there was some family issue that would help explain Logan's disappearance, they would have said something to him by now.

It was a frustrating situation all around and every avenue of inquiry seemed to lead to a dead end. The phone lines had been checked and there had been no unusual incoming or outgoing calls. The computer was clean and no one in the neighborhood had seen anything. It was as if Logan had simply vanished into thin air.

"Uncle Brian?" Lt. Sweeney heard someone softly call his name and his head snapped up. He saw Ryan standing in the doorway of the Michaud's family room, anxiously looking over at him.

Lt. Sweeney rose from the chair he was sitting in and walked over.

"What is it, Ryan?" he asked.

"I just came over to see . . . I mean, I didn't know if there was anything . . ." Ryan stammered. "The door was open so I just walked in," he added lamely.

"It's okay, Ryan. The door's unlocked so people can come and go."

"Have they found . . . him?" Ryan whispered.

Lt. Sweeney slowly shook his head; then he glanced back at Anne Michaud still sitting on the sofa staring dumbly at the carpet.

He turned and led Ryan back into the hallway, "Did Logan say anything to you about wanting to leave West Bend? Maybe wanting to go back to Canada to see friends or something?"

139

"No, nothing like that," Ryan answered. "In fact, he talked about moving around a lot, so I got the impression there was no particular place that was, you know, more special than any other."

"Was there anyone at school he was having problems with?"

Ryan thought back to Tyler's initial dislike of Logan. But that had been minor stuff and things were better now, especially since the team was winning, so he shook his head and said, "No, no one."

"And he never talked about going online to chat rooms or talking to strangers on the Internet?"

Ryan emphatically shook his head no. "Really, we mostly skateboarded over at the skate park or came back here and played video games."

"Did you ever meet anyone at the skate park who seemed suspicious or like they didn't belong?"

"Never. It's usually just a bunch of kids from the middle school and maybe a few high schoolers. No one I didn't recognize."

But his uncle's use of the word "suspicious" triggered something in Ryan's brain and his eyes widened slightly as a thought occurred to him.

"Actually, there *was* one thing we talked about..." he started to say.

"What was it?" his uncle asked quickly, his face suddenly alert.

"Well, it's just that . . . Logan seemed to think there was something weird going on at that car repair shop on Locust Street. You know, the one on the corner. I think it's called Exotic Cars or something."

"What do you mean weird?"

Ryan was quiet for a moment and then he snapped his fingers. "Yeah, I remember now. Logan told me that one night Joker had to go outside really late and so Logan let him out. He ran into the woods behind the house and when Logan chased after him, he saw a car drive up and a guy got out and someone came out of that Exotic place and handed the driver some cash. Or Logan thought it was cash."

"When was this?"

"It was weeks ago, I think, but Logan thought the guy looked like a gangbanger or something."

"How late was it?"

"Actually it was more like really early in the morning, maybe 3:00 a.m. or something. I remember telling Logan I couldn't believe he was tromping through the woods at that hour. I would have been scared to death, but of course he had Joker."

Lt. Sweeney was already jotting notes down in a small notebook. "Anything else you can think of?"

"Well, last weekend after the game against the Ice Dogs, we were skateboarding around the neighborhood and we snuck over behind the place. We were just goofing around and stuff. Logan peeked in their dumpster, but there was nothing in there but garbage. Then, one of the guys came out to smoke a cigarette in the alley and we hid behind a fence."

"Did he see you?"

"No, I'm sure he didn't, but he was wearing a big apron with paint splatters on it and he had one of those white masks hanging around his neck. And we could see inside the building and there were spray guns hanging down and pieces of cars, like car doors, on tables."

"Did you see anything suspicious?"

"No, that's the thing. I remember telling Logan it's not illegal to paint cars and that's what it looked like these guys were doing. But Logan thought the guy looked like he belonged in a prison 'cause he had tattoos all over his arms."

Ryan was shaking his head, "I asked Logan if he wanted to say something to you, but he said no, that it was probably just his imagination."

Then Ryan added, "The other thing Logan thought was weird was the big metal fence they have around the building. But we both figured they needed the extra security because of the expensive sports cars they work on. You know, Porsches and Ferraris and stuff."

At the mention of the word Ferrari, Lt. Sweeney's head jerked up and he stopped writing in his notebook. Pulling his cellphone from his pocket, he punched a button and started barking orders to someone on the other end.

"I need whatever background information you can get on that auto shop on Locust. Yeah, I think it's called Exotic Cars or something. And I need it stat," he said as he rushed down the hallway towards the front door.

Chapter 23

Skinny guy and Frankie were taking a dinner break and watching television when they heard the loud knock on the door.

According to the clock, it was 6:35 p.m. and the sun's rays were slanting sideways through the skylights, casting shadows in the center garage area. The space had grown dark without the overhead lights on, but Logan didn't mind. In fact, he felt safer in the darkness, like a small mouse hiding in his mousehole.

The sound startled the two men who looked at each other, surprise clearly written on their faces. For a moment they seemed paralyzed with uncertainty, but then skinny guy got up and walked out of the office towards the side door. Suddenly another series of knocks sounded and his head swiveled around to stare at the front of the building.

It sounds like someone's at the front door, Logan thought. And he probably realizes it's not someone he knows because anyone he knows would come up the driveway and use the other door.

Putting a finger to his lips, skinny guy signaled to Frankie to be quiet. Then he motioned for Frankie to head to the back of the shop and Frankie took off in the direction of the back hallway.

There was a third knock and this time the person knocking sounded very insistent. Skinny guy reached into a desk drawer and pulled out something black and solid and slipped it into the pocket of his jacket. Then he walked briskly in the direction of the sounds.

Meanwhile Lt. Sweeney and another uniformed officer were standing outside the front door of Exotic Auto. There was another squad car parked out of sight at the end of the alley and a third car positioned a block and a half down the street. In addition, there were numerous police officers on foot at various points around the building, including two policemen behind the alley fence where Logan and Ryan had hidden.

Lt. Sweeney had decided on a low-key and nonthreatening approach, not wanting to alert those inside to the fact that they were under surveillance. The background check hadn't revealed any definitive link to known criminal associates, but Lt. Sweeney had a gut feeling something wasn't right.

There was a truck parked in the enclosed yard, so he was confident someone was inside, but despite his knocking, no one had come to the door. Finally after he pounded on the door for the third time, he heard the sounds of shuffling feet from inside.

A tall skinny man with scraggly long hair and dirty jeans opened the door partway.

"Yeah?" he asked, a sullen expression on his face.

"Do you mind if we come it?" Lt. Sweeney asked politely.

"I don't mind, but the owner might," the guy answered. "What d'ya want?"

Lt. Sweeney had carefully planned what he would say to whoever answered the door. He pulled out a picture of Logan from a folder he was carrying and watched the man's face closely as he said, "There's a young boy in the neighborhood who's gone missing and we're going door-to-door, checking to see if anyone's seen him."

Lt. Sweeney extended the picture, but the guy didn't make a move to take it and, in fact, barely glanced at it.

"Nah, I ain't seen no kid," the guy said.

"Maybe if you looked a little closer at the picture, you might be able to recognize him if he does show up."

Reluctantly, skinny guy looked down at the picture of Logan's smiling face, but still his eyes displayed no sign of recognition.

"Nope, never seen him before," he said.

"Is there anyone else inside that we could talk to?" Lt. Sweeney persisted.

The guy looked over his shoulder and then back at the police officers, as if making up his mind about something. He opened the door a little wider and snatched the picture out of Lt. Sweeney's hand.

"Wait here," he said, shutting the door in the officers' faces.

As Lt. Sweeney waited quietly outside on the front steps, he heard the sound of barking in the distance. Turning, he saw a dark form burst from the woods across the street and streak across the roadway directly towards him. As the shape drew closer, he recognized the brown and black coloring of Logan's dog, Joker, who bounded up to meet him, his body quivering with agitation.

Lt. Sweeney was reaching down to quiet the excited dog just as skinny guy returned. "Is that a police dog?" he asked, eyeing Joker who had started to growl low in his throat.

"Hold on, boy," Lt. Sweeney said soothingly. He grabbed Joker by the collar to restrain him.

Skinny guy opened the door a little wider to hand the picture back. "Nobody here's seen this . . . " he started to say, but he never got a chance to finish his sentence. Seeing the door widen, Joker lunged forward and broke free of Lt. Sweeney's grasp. Within seconds, he had flashed by skinny guy and was racing into the garage barking furiously.

From his hiding place in the storage room, Logan recognized the sound of his dog's bark and pushed himself up off the ground. His legs were stiff and awkward from having been bent for so long. Stumbling to the door, he saw skinny guy chasing Joker into the garage with Coach Sweeney and another police officer a few steps behind in hot pursuit.

"Hey!" skinny guy yelled when he saw Logan standing in the doorway clutching the frame for support. Then his face contorted into an angry mask.

Logan heard someone yell stop and watched as skinny guy reached into his pocket and start to pull something out.

"He's got a gun!" Logan shouted.

He heard Joker growl and saw him turn back around. And just as he watched his dog launch himself at skinny guy, Logan heard the sharp crack of a gunshot.

Chapter 24

The two officers in the alley tackled Frankie as soon as he burst through the alley door. Once he'd heard the commotion in the garage, Frankie figured it was every man for himself so he hadn't bothered to wait for further instructions from his partner and had tried to make his own escape out back.

When the other officers arrived on the scene, they found both men handcuffed on the floor of the garage. Frankie was subdued but skinny guy was screaming his head off about how the police better make sure they kept that rabid dog away from him or else they'd be facing a lawsuit. The stray bullet fired from skinny guy's gun had grazed Joker's shoulder and one of the officers with medical training had examined the wound and declared it to be a superficial scratch.

Joker for his part seemed oblivious to his injury – he was too busy trying to jump up and lick Logan's face, he was so happy to see him.

Hours later, Logan sat down for his first meal of the day. Even though it was well past 10:00 p.m., his mom had made him a breakfast meal of pancakes and bacon, and despite the exhaustion he was feeling, he wolfed it down. He had received a stern lecture from his mom about the foolishness of his actions, but there was nothing she'd said to him that he hadn't already said a million times to himself while hiding in the storage closet. He knew he'd done a stupid thing by sneaking into the auto shop by himself. There was a world of difference between chasing an imaginary bad guy on a video screen and coming face-to-face with one in real life. From now on he'd let the real police do the detective work. But like everyone else, his mom was so happy to see him safe and sound, she couldn't bring herself to stay angry with him for too long.

Lying at Logan's feet and watching his owner's every move lest he try to slip away again, Joker was wearing his badge of courage – a big white bandage – on his left shoulder. He hadn't wanted to leave Logan even for a second so everyone had trooped over to the animal hospital together while the veterinarian patched him up.

Then Logan had spent a long time being interviewed by Lt. Sweeney and another officer about what had transpired that day. Preliminary reports indicated that Frankie and skinny guy were both ex-cons and neither was authorized to carry a weapon of any kind. Moreover, after running the license plate number of the Ferrari, it turned out the car had been reported stolen in Florida, so both men were charged with receipt of stolen property. The combination of these offenses was enough to hold the men in custody while the police continued their investigation. In addition to seizing computer records, the police were also following up on a stack of 18 license plates that had been found stuffed in a drawer in one of the offices. Lt. Sweeney told Logan they figured the owner of the shop was running an auto theft ring that specialized in stealing and reselling high-end sports cars.

Ryan sent word through his uncle that he was happy Logan was safe and that he'd see him at the game tomorrow. The Warriors were scheduled to play the Bears on Sunday at 1:00 p.m., and despite a request from Coach Sweeney to reschedule the game, the other coach refused. He told Coach Sweeney if his team didn't show up at the rink, they'd have to forfeit.

Logan had no intention of letting that happen, so he told Coach Sweeney he'd be there for sure. By the time he crawled into bed at the end of a very eventful day, he had been awake for almost 19 hours straight. And even though he'd spent most of that time hiding in a pile of drop cloths, his body was exhausted from the constant tension of wondering if and when he'd be discovered. As soon as his head hit the pillow, Logan fell into a deep and dreamless sleep.

Chapter 25

The complex where the Bears skated was a brand new facility with two full sheets of ice, a large pro shop, a sit-down restaurant serving burgers and beer and an exercise area for off-ice training. The drive to the rink took 45 minutes and Logan arrived an hour before game time. When he walked in the locker room, his teammates greeted him with some good-natured ribbing, some even calling him Logan Michaud, Boy Spy.

"I can't believe you actually snuck into that building," Ryan said, as he wound black tape around the bottom of his stick.

"Yeah, it was dumb," Logan agreed. "But I just kept thinking that all I needed was that license plate number. I was so sure those guys were shady."

"Well, you were right about that. You know, my uncle said something about there being a Crime Stoppers Reward Fund you might be eligible for. I guess if an ordinary citizen or whatever gives the police a tip and it leads to an arrest, they sometimes pay a reward, like $1,000 or more."

Logan grinned. "I'll take it. I can apply it to next year's hockey fees."

"Trust me, Logan. If you need money for next year, the team's prepared to take up a collection."

Coach Brian stopped by the locker room to say a few words before the game.

"Just remember," he said. "This is a physical team, so you guys need to play physical too. But that doesn't mean getting stupid penalties."

"Uh oh," Carlos said. "I think he's looking at you, Tyler," and loud guffaws of laughter filled the Warriors' locker room.

Skating out for the opening face-off, Logan knew he wasn't feeling one hundred percent, either physically or mentally. His legs were still tired from the strain of the previous day and his brain was feeling sluggish. During his first few shifts, he seemed to be chasing the puck around the ice rather than playing his position smartly.

Then as he tried to dig out a puck that one of his defensemen had wrapped around the back of the net, a Bears player leveled him. Much to the vocal disappointment of the Warriors' fans, the referee didn't blow his whistle and Logan, slow to get up, skated back to the bench. As Logan sat down wearily, his head bowed, Tyler leaned over and said, "They're gunning for you, Logan. You better watch your back."

Coach Brian sat Logan for the next few shifts to make sure he was all right and it didn't take long for the Bears' number one line to score their first goal. Luke Frankel positioned himself in his usual spot right in front of the net and slapped in a rebound that skittered away from the goalie, Brad Lyman, before he could get his glove on it.

Suddenly the huge scoreboard in the rink exploded into a swirling kaleidoscope of bright colors. The word "SCORE" flashed on the screen and the sound system began to play a victory march. Then a professional-style announcer intoned the name and number of the player who had scored the goal.

"NUUMMMBERRR 23, LUKE FFFRANKELLL."

It was all a bit too much for Logan who looked over and saw the Bears' bench celebrating with high fives and fist bumps. He could feel the anger start to burn in his gut, fueling his competitive spirit.

Logan saw the Bears' second line skate out to take the face-off at center ice, and sensing an opportunity, he quickly turned to Coach Brian and said, "I'm ready to go back in, Coach. I feel fine."

Coach Brian nodded and Logan vaulted over the low rink wall and skated out to the red line. Carlos was at the center spot and Tyler and James were back on defense. Logan edged over to Tyler and said in a low voice, "If you can, try to get me a stretch pass down the right side."

Carlos got his stick on the puck first and was able to shovel it back to Tyler who then forwarded it to the Warriors' left winger along the boards. The forward tried to skate it up but he didn't get more than 10 feet before a Bears player crashed into him and stripped him of the puck. The Bears then reversed direction and charged up the ice in unison. Once the Bears' stickhandler crossed the centerline, he dumped the puck into the corner and chased after it.

As the Warriors defensemen and the Bears forwards battled for possession behind the Warriors' net, Logan crisscrossed in front, constantly moving his body but drifting closer and closer to the blue line. Logan could see Tyler working hard to muscle the puck away from the other team. Three players were tangled up along the boards, each one trying to poke the puck loose. Finally it slipped out and Tyler was there to grab it. He looked up and saw Logan start to streak up the ice. Within seconds Logan was behind the Bears' defenseman who had pinched in too close.

Tyler's pass was right on the money, just far enough ahead of Logan that he didn't have to break stride to catch it. The Warriors' fans were on their feet, cheering him on.

Logan had nothing but clear ice in front of him. He could see the Bears' goalie square himself in the center of the net and raise his goalie glove. He remembered how impressive the Bears' goalie had been in the earlier match against the Warriors, always able to sense the moves of the players in front of him.

I can't be too obvious, Logan thought.

Then Logan remembered a move his dad had taught him when he was younger. His dad had called it his "signature move." Rather than commit to one side too soon, the idea was to head straight at the goalie, and at the last possible second swoop left, then cut right and fire the puck hard, making sure to keep it elevated. It's easier for the goalie to move from one side of the net to the other – his dad had said – than it is for him to start at center, move left and then have to move right. And remember to elevate the puck, his dad had told him, because the goalie's first instinct is to stop the low shot.

As Logan bore down on the net, he forced himself to head for the center of the goal. When he was almost on top of the goalie, he suddenly veered left and then right, and the last thing he saw as he flew by was the round shape of the black puck sailing over the goalie's arm into the white netting.

Goal!

Logan celebrated with a double fist pump, and Tyler raced over and gave him at spirited pat on the head.

"Great shot!" he said, grinning widely.

"Great pass!" Logan answered, smiling back.

As he skated back to the bench with his linemates, Logan's mind was working overtime.

That Frankel kids is strong, but he mostly just plants himself in front of the net and looks for rebounds, Logan thought. If our defensemen push him out of position, we can neutralize him and then look to score on some of the weaker lines.

The tiredness Logan had felt earlier seemed to magically disappear.

Yeah, he thought, nodding to himself. We can beat this team. I know we can.

Made in the USA
San Bernardino, CA
19 January 2014